D1621770

A CAT AND HIS DOGS

OTHER BOOKS BY KURT UNKELBACH

Ruffian: *International Champion*
Murphy
The Dog Who Never Knew
Love on a Leash
The Winning of Westminster
The Dog in My Life
Both Ends of the Leash: *Selecting and Training Your Dog*

A
CAT
AND HIS
DOGS

By

Kurt Unkelbach

Illustrated by Shannon Stirnweis

*Based on the story of a real
cat and his associates—animal and human*

PRENTICE-HALL, INC., ENGLEWOOD CLIFFS, N.J.

A CAT AND HIS DOGS by Kurt Unkelbach

13-120774-1

Library of Congress Catalog Card Number: 69-15834

Printed in the United States of America   ·   J

Prentice-Hall International, Inc., London
Prentice-Hall of Australia, Pty. Ltd., Sydney
Prentice-Hall of Canada, Ltd., Toronto
Prentice-Hall of India Private Ltd., New Delhi
Prentice-Hall of Japan, Inc., Tokyo

This story of a real cat and
his associates — animal and human —
is dedicated to Janet Mack

CONTENTS

1

THE CHRISTMAS PLOT

THE new boy in school was big for his age—so big and strong that he towered over Cary and all his other classmates in the eighth grade, and the freshman football coach at high school was already eyeing him as a potential fullback. William S. Hall was the boy's name. He arrived in early November, and within days everyone knew that he was a brilliant student.

This didn't keep him from becoming popular with the other boys in the class. They liked him from the start, and they were willing to overlook the fact that he was the only one among them who still wore a crew cut. The girls appreciated him just as much as the teachers, for he was mannerly and always neatly dressed. Indeed, the teachers wished that a few of the other boys would use him as a model for themselves.

Billy Hall was almost too good to be true, but only one person suspected this. Her name was Cary, and she and Billy occupied adjoining desks in homeroom. And by chance, they also found themselves sitting together on the school bus almost every day.

By the end of that first week, Cary had discovered something about Billy that made her wonder if he wasn't something of an oddball: Billy loved cats.

"Maybe *lost* is a better word than *love*," Cary confided to Sally, one of her best friends. "He's lost in cats." And later she reported to her mother: "He's a walking encyclopedia on the subject of *Felis catus*."

"Replay that, please," requested Mom. "Who is what?"

"Billy Hall, the new boy at school. I've told you about him, remember? Well, he doesn't say much in class, but on the bus he talks and talks about cats. Ever hear of Manx cats? From the Isle of Man? They don't have tails."

"I know. I owned one when I was about your age," said Mom. "Do you have time to feed the puppies? The food is mixed."

The question was also a command, for the day was a Saturday and Cary had plenty of time. As she watched the seven yellow pups dive into their food and gulp it down, Cary thought back over the week and concluded that it had been one of surprises.

First: Billy Hall. He was the first cat-loving member of the opposite sex, man or boy, she'd ever met. Somehow, it didn't seem right to her that a boy should prefer cats over other pets—especially over dogs. She noticed that one of the pups was sitting in the middle of the feeding pan, and as she picked him up she asked, "Billy Hall is a cat fancier, now what do you think of that?" The pup, as if in reply, chewed on her right thumb.

Second: Mom. The news that her very own mother had once owned a cat was perhaps an even bigger surprise. Cary was sure that Mom had loved that cat, although now she was an ardent dog fancier and had been one for as long as her daughter could remember. Perhaps ardent wasn't a strong enough word, for Mom was a breeder of Labrador Retrievers and owned Walden Kennels. It was a hobby kennel, but it required as much work as a business. And for years Cary had been the unsalaried kennel maid, and as devoted a dog fancier as her mother.

When the pups were through eating, Cary removed the pan and played with them for a few minutes. She sat down in the kennel run and they climbed over her lap, tugged at her shoe laces, and tried to eat her shoes. She laughed and patted them, but her mind was still on Billy and cats and mothers and dogs, and all the thinking led to a decision. When she left the pups, she told them. "It's chance, you see. I'm a dog fancier because my mother is one. Billy's a cat fancier because his mother is one. She's always had a cattery, and it dates back to before he was born. If she had an elephanttery, he'd be an elephant fancier. A matter of early environment."

The pups barked and yipped as they watched her go back to the house. Their bellies were full but they wanted more to eat, and they were telling her. Cary preferred to regard their noise as applause for her humor.

She found her mother in the kitchen, mixing food for the five house dogs. The big Labs, four yellows and a black, were sitting in a semicircle, expressions serious and eyes intent on every move that Mom made. Not one of them—not even Champion Thumper of Walden, Cary's own dog—glanced at the girl as she came into the house and asked, "What was his name?"

"Name? Whose name?"

"The name of the Manx cat you owned."

"Oh. Her name was Pansy," said Mom. "You don't see that breed very often."

"Billy's mother raises them. They have Himalayans and Russian Blues, too. Why is it that we've never owned a cat?"

Mom was busy slicing pieces of suet and adding it to the dogs' dishes. "Don't tell your father," she said. "He bought this suet for the songbirds, but there's nothing like it for dogs' coats. Well, I've thought about a cat from time to time. The moles ruin the lawn and garden, and the mice think they own the attic. So a cat would be a practical addition to the family. On the other hand, your father complains enough about the cost of feeding so many dogs."

"It wouldn't cost much to feed a cat," commented Cary.

"You miss the point. He likes dogs, so he's tolerant about their overhead. On the other hand, he hates cats."

"Why?"

"It's one of the world's great mysteries," Mom explained. "Most men don't like cats. How many boys in your school own dogs, and how many own cats? The truth is that the majority of the men who like cats are married to women who love cats. The exceptions are usually city bachelors who are too lazy to walk dogs but want some sort of pet. Do you have time to feed the house dogs?"

In the thirteen years of her life, Cary had owned a variety of pets: rabbits, hamsters, a parrot, a goat, a descented skunk, ducks, and several dogs. For three years she had been campaigning for a horse, but this wish had not been fulfilled. She didn't see it that way, but a horse would have been impractical at Walden, where the house sat high on a twenty-acre mountain and the land was sharply graded. In addition, the property was wooded, and hundreds of trees would have had to come down to create even a minimum of sloping pasture. Physically, the place wasn't right for a horse.

Cary still retained the wish, although she knew it was futile. But the landscape that wasn't right for a horse would be no trouble at all for a cat. So despite a feeling of guilt, she started wondering about owning a cat.

The guilty feeling wasn't strong and it disappeared in a few days. The guilt was there because of her love for dogs. Would Thumper and all the other dogs look upon her wish for a cat as treason? Can a dog lover be a cat lover, too?

This new wish wasn't a sudden thing. It sort of grew on her, and the daily, cat-oriented conversations with Billy Hall helped the growth. His was the voice of experience, particularly because the Hall family's animal population included two dogs: a Miniature Poodle and a Shetland Sheepdog. Most authorities agree that those two breeds are among the smartest on earth, but Billy—while admitting their intelligence—thought them less wise than cats and certainly far less interesting. "I like dogs, and I don't mean to downgrade them," he explained, "but their intelligence and capabilities are so limited. I think of the cat as the most interesting and talented animal on earth. Would you like one?"

"I don't mean to downgrade cats," Cary told him, "but my father dislikes them."

That ended that conversation. But Billy was dedicated to the proposition that no one can lead a full life without a cat, and two days later—as they sat together on the school bus—he asked, "Were you kidding about your father? Does he really dislike cats?"

"You have my mother's word for it."

"And what about her?"

"Mom? Oh, she likes cats. She owned a Manx when she was a girl."

Billy grinned and said, "Then your problem is solved."

"Problem? I don't have any problem," announced Cary.

"Oh, yes, you do. We intend to give you a kitten for Christmas, but not over the objections of your father. A kitten deserves a happy home."

Cary waited for him to say more, but he didn't. The school bus stopped at the front gates of Walden. Cary nodded to Billy, stepped off the bus, and started walking up the long, steep drive to the house. Thumper was usually there to meet her, but not on this day. Cary wondered if he suspected she was thinking about owning a cat.

She passed the kennel building. The pups saw her first and yipped at her, and then the adult dogs started barking. She waved at all of them but didn't stop. The kennel bedlam continued until she disappeared into the house.

Mom was preparing the fourth and last meal of the day for the pups. "I thought you were the arrival," was her greeting. "The barks are louder when a stranger comes along. I'm late feeding the pups because I had a visitor this afternoon, thanks to you."

"Oh? Who?"

"Does the name Thelma Hall ring a bell?"

"No," said Cary. "Should it? A long lost cousin of Pop's?"

"This one is the mother of a young man named

Billy Hall," Mom explained. "If she's long lost, she's long lost only in cats. She was here for over an hour, and I'm afraid I made a very weak impression. It seems I used poor judgment in marrying a man who doesn't like cats."

"She said that?"

"Not in so many words, but she implied it," Mom explained. "Well, it seems that Billy wants to give you a kitten for Christmas. A Russian Blue, no less! One hundred dollars worth of kitten. I had no idea purebred cats cost so much. Times have changed. Did you know anything about this kitten?"

Cary nodded yes. "Billy told me on the school bus today. He didn't mention anything about his mother coming to see you. I'm sorry."

"Don't be. I like to know that every pup we sell is going to a home where every member of the family will love him. Do you really want a cat, Cary? As much as a horse, I mean?"

Cary sat down and studied her mother's face for a long moment before asking, "Is there any chance of a horse?"

"I'm afraid not."

"Then I might as well try for a cat. To tell the truth, I've been thinking more and more about cats. Billy makes them sound so interesting. But what will Pop say?"

Mom shrugged, sighed, and then said, "Well, twenty shopping days until Christmas, or twenty days for us to change his mind. It won't be easy, for he can be stubborn. Maybe the Christmas spirit will help. And let's not forget that once upon a time he was a dedicated bachelor. He changed his mind about that."

Cary laughed and left her chair to kiss her mother's cheek. "I'll get into some old clothes now," she said.

"Your father will be home early. I must get busy on dinner. If you can find the time, would you mind feeding the pups and taking fresh water to the kennel dogs?"

During dinner on the evening when there were just fifteen shopping days left before Christmas, Cary broke the silence around the table by remarking, "I learned something new at school today. Did either of you know that the ancient Egyptians worshiped the cat?"

"I didn't," said Mom. "How long ago was that?"

"About five thousand years ago. And they had a goddess named Pasht. She had the body of a woman and the head of a cat."

"How interesting! Why, that's fascinating! Don't you think so?" asked Mom, directing her question to the head of the house.

"Ancient history is always interesting, and we can always learn something from it," was Pop's advice. "Among other forms of life, the ancient Egyptians also worshiped the dog, the crocodile, and the baboon. And look at Egypt today. Let that be a lesson to both of you!" He laughed, but the ladies didn't join him.

Cary waited until dinner was almost over before broaching the cat subject again. "Another thing I learned is that the dog and the cat have a common ancestor. Millions of years ago, of course."

"Are they teaching zoology in the eighth grade these days?" asked Pop. "No, don't tell me. Biology?"

"There's a new boy in my class at school. Billy Hall. He's sort of a cat authority, and he's been telling me about them," Cary explained.

"Oh, yes. His family moved here from Ohio about a month ago," said Pop. "I know his father. He's on my morning train to the city."

"What's he like?" asked Mom.

"Hard to say. He's the quiet type. Spends most of the trip gazing out the window. A nice enough fellow, but he has the unhappiest look I've ever seen on the face of a man. When I see him on the night train coming home, he looks even gloomier. Say, did you sell any pups today?"

"I haven't advertised them yet," his wife reminded him. "They're only seven weeks old."

The conversation didn't swing back to cats again, and Cary was thankful. It was not the time to explain that the Halls had a cattery, for Pop might assume that Mr. Hall's unhappiness was due to too many cats.

Hours later, when the house was in total darkness

and everybody—dogs and people—should have been asleep, Mom asked, "Are you asleep?"

"Yes," replied her husband. "Why?"

"I was thinking about Christmas."

"Same here. I still don't know what to get you."

"I was thinking about the big gift for Cary," Mom explained. "She's been dropping hints."

"Don't tell me, let me guess." He paused, then asked, "A horse, of course?"

"Yes, but this year we have an alternative. A horse or something else, and I'm not sure I should tell you what the something else is." She waited for him to ask—and when he didn't, she asked, "Are you awake?"

"No, but tell me anyway. What's the alternative to a horse?"

"I thought you might have guessed from her talk at dinner tonight."

"Let me think," said Pop. "Well, now, I don't know why she'd want an ancient Egyptian." He thought some more before groaning, then asked, "A cat? No, no, she wouldn't do that to me! Not a cat!" And when his wife didn't reply, he asked again, "A cat? Say, are you asleep?"

"I'm awake, and Cary wants a cat. I was afraid you wouldn't like the idea."

"You know how I feel about cats," he continued. "Why, I'm surprised you even mentioned this to me. Look at it this way: If you disliked hippopotamuses and Cary wanted a hippo, I'd tell her she couldn't have one!"

Mom had to laugh. His rationalization was that silly.

"This is not a laughing matter. I don't think I could live in a house with a cat. I hate the darn things. And listen, I have enough trouble as it is trying to walk around here without stumbling over a dog. I'm lucky to be alive! And sure as sin, I'd step on a cat and break its neck and mine! And what about the birds?"

"Birds?" murmured Mom.

"The songbirds. I thought this family loved birds. Why, we've created a paradise for them. Feeders and nest boxes everywhere. More birds and more varieties every year. Do you know what a cat would do to our fine feathered friends? I think that's why I hate cats."

Mom didn't say anything. She was asleep.

When he realized that fact, Pop tried to go to sleep himself. But his mind was on cats, and he was still awake twenty minutes later. Thinking that a cup of warm milk might help bring sleep, he got out of bed and almost stumbled over the sleeping body of old Duke. Then Pop groped his way through the darkness to the bedroom door, where he did step on Folly. She whacked her tail against the floor, forgiving him. Finally, he made his way to the kitchen.

At the precise moment that he switched on the kitchen light, Cary was asleep and dreaming. The dream was one that she would remember the following morning. In it, Billy Hall presented her with a Russian Blue kitten, and he explained that she would have to learn to speak Russian, or the kitten wouldn't understand her commands.

"He's being difficult," Mom reported the next day. "It won't be as easy to convince him as I thought. You know how he feels about the songbirds."

"But not every cat wants to kill birds," Cary reminded her. "Why, Sally's cat lets the canary sit on his head. What were Pop's other objections?"

"I don't know. I fell asleep."

"Maybe there's a way to train cats not to go after birds. I'll ask Billy."

From Billy, Cary learned that you just can't predict anything about a given cat. "Some will go for birds, and some will show no interest in them," was his solemn analysis. "About the only thing you can do with a cat who's determined to hunt birds is to keep him indoors. Otherwise, you can always hang a bell around his neck, as a warning to the birds. But a smart cat soon learns to overcome that handicap. He's a patient animal, and he just waits for the bird to come a little closer before he leaps." But Billy did have some cheerful news: "You can assure your father that I have never known a Russian Blue who wanted to hunt birds."

The news cheered Cary, but not Mom. "Your father is sure to point out that Billy doesn't know all the Russian Blues in the world. But I'll tell him anyway. What did Billy say about dogs?"

"Not a thing. Why?"

"Well, you know how most dogs are about cats. Your father will undoubtedly think of that. Would our dogs accept a cat? Or would we have one war after another?"

"I don't think an adult dog would harm a kitten," said Cary. "I'll get Billy's opinion tomorrow."

She was correct. Billy assured her that while adult dogs are not as smart as cats, the dogs have just enough brains to recognize a kitten as a harmless, defenseless baby. "And a grown cat won't go after a little puppy," the boy added. "By the way, I've prepared a list of names for you."

"Names?" asked Cary, as she accepted the piece of paper he offered to her. Billy had written such names as Mark Twain, Theodore Roosevelt, Winston Churchill, Babe Ruth, Charles Dickens, and Edgar Allan Poe. And there were more. In all, Billy had a list of over thirty famous men. Cary was puzzled, but not for long.

"Every one of those men held the cat in high esteem," Billy explained. "They were all cat lovers, although I'm not sure of Babe Ruth. I put his name down because he was probably one of your father's first heroes. Do you get the message?"

Cary grinned and nodded. "Never mind Babe Ruth," she said. "Are you sure about Theodore Roosevelt?"

"Of course. Why, he was the first President to have a cat in the White House."

"This might work," said Cary. "My father thinks that Teddy Roosevelt was one of the great men of history."

"It worked with my father," Billy told her. "He changed his mind about cats when my mother told him about Edgar Allan Poe."

"I'll try it on my father tonight," Cary promised.

But Cary didn't keep the promise. It seemed wise to consult Mom about the plan of action, and as a result the plan was changed.

"I'm afraid it will seem too obvious if it comes from you," Mom decided. "Better let me handle it. I'll get him talking about Teddy Roosevelt, and then I'll spring this news. Unless I'm sadly mistaken, your father will change his mind about cats. As far as he's concerned, Teddy Roosevelt was the perfect man."

Somehow, Mom knew that she wouldn't be able to keep a straight face when she brought up the subject, so she waited until bedtime. Then, when the lights were out and her husband couldn't see her face, she said, "Speaking of Teddy Roosevelt. . . ."

After a few moments of silence, Pop asked, "Who was?"

"Who was what?"

"Who was speaking of Teddy Roosevelt? I didn't hear anybody."

"Sorry. I must have been thinking out loud,"

Mom said. "Cary is studying him in American History."

"Again? She studied him last year. What sort of a school is this?"

"She says the teacher insists that he was a very great man."

"Just what I've been saying for years," Pop reminded her. "Teddy was one of the great men of history, and the greatest American who ever lived!"

"Did you know that he loved cats?" asked Mom. She waited, and when there was no answer she asked again, "Did you know that? He adored cats. He even had one with him in the White House!"

"I didn't know that," Pop admitted. "Are you sure?"

"Very sure. And he wasn't the only great man who liked cats. What about Winston Churchill, John Jacob Astor, Mark Twain, Victor Hugo, Babe Ruth? Now, don't you feel a little silly?"

"Not at all," replied Pop. "You are simply proving that even the great have their weaknesses. Goodnight."

Old Duke banged his tail against the floor and groaned. The dog was curled up on the rug on Pop's side of the bed, and he was asking for quiet so that he could sleep. He got it.

It was the end of the plot to secure a Christmas kitten for Cary: Big Wind, the family's favorite name for the president of Pop's firm, decided to send Pop on a business trip to Mexico City.

There was no opportunity to bring up the case of the kitten again. A company car picked up Pop and delivered him to the airport. He was gone before Cary arrived home from school, and her first question was about the Russian Blue. "Did he change his mind about the kitten?"

"No," said Mom. "The kitten was the last thing he had on his mind. I'm sorry, but we're a couple of failures. And your father is a very stubborn man."

Cary nodded, then smiled and said, "I'm like him. I'm stubborn, too."

"Now what does that mean? You can't disobey him about this kitten!"

"I know. I'll forget about Christmas and start working on my birthday."

Her mother laughed and then hugged her. The hug was really a silent pledge of cooperation, and Cary understood it that way. Together they would somehow change Pop's mind before her next birthday.

Neither of them knew that the first deep snow of winter would cover the ground within a few days, and that the snow would prove more effective than their combined schemes and dreams.

2

GIFT FROM A STRANGER

POP was the only one who didn't mind the storm. He was far off in sunny Mexico when the Arctic air blew in from the northwest and the dark sky tumbled out its snow. At the end of three days the winds died down to occasional gusts and the sun peeked through the clouds.

Walden looked as pretty as a picture postcard. The white blanket was four feet deep, and more than that where the winds had drifted the snow. The birches and saplings were bent to the ground under the weight of their snow-laden branches. It was a beautiful scene, but it meant work. Mom had to attach the plow to the jeep and clear out the long driveway every day, and then she and Cary had to

19

shovel a path to the kennel, and then shovel the snow from the kennel runs. The dogs and the pups weren't able to help.

And all of the cold beauty spelled trouble for the wildlife in the woods, for their food supplies were buried under the snow. Only the fat raccoons were content. They stayed in their favorite tree hollows, sleeping most of the time and avoiding any exertion that might make them hungry. But the deer and the foxes and the rabbits kept on the move, hoping to find nourishment and not having much luck. Still, they were true creatures of the wild, and most would somehow survive.

The only animal in real trouble was the half-wild one: a jet black cat who had discovered the Walden woods weeks before and decided that the setting was just right as a home base for her soon-to-be family. She was a stray and just over seven months old— too young to have known the previous winter, but old enough to be a mother. Billy Hall would have called her a queen, the human term for a mother cat.

This queen had given birth to three kittens, and all during the storm she'd stayed with them in the nest, nursing them and keeping them warm. The nest was hidden away under the massive, rotted trunk of a fallen white oak, and neither the winds nor the snow had reached it. The kittens were almost a month old and just able to move about under their own power, and just beginning to know hunger for the first time. Their mother had not

been able to hunt for food during the storm, and
her supply of milk had run dry. Her children were
complaining.

The queen was desperate. She needed food for
herself and her little ones, but she'd never hunted
in snow before and couldn't find what she was looking for: field mice and chipmunks, her regular diet.
Squirrels, both the red and the gray, were staying
high off the ground, and they saw her long before
she spotted them. Time spent pursuing them would
have been in vain, and they weren't about to come
within leaping distance of her.

And now she couldn't wander far from the nest.
The kittens might try to follow her and become lost
in the sea of white stuff. And they were talking, telling the world where their hidden nest was, and that
was dangerous. So the queen had to hunt, but she
had to remain close. As a result, she and her new
family continued to go hungry. Finally there came a
time when she had to risk traveling a greater distance from the nest. There was food somewhere, and
she was determined to find it.

But when she did find some food there was nothing she could do about procuring it. On that late
afternoon she could only watch from the woods as a
girl placed five dishes on a path near a house, and
then watch some more as five dogs devoured the
food.

When darkness came, the queen worked her way
through the snow toward the house. She searched
out the area where the dishes had been and found

just a few pieces of kibble biscuit scattered on the path. She ate the kibble, then retreated to the woods and started the long journey back to the nest under the fallen trunk.

The kittens were making more noise than ever before. The queen heard them and covered the last hundred feet in a hurry, for to her their voices came from fear as well as hunger.

She was right. The nest contained two kittens. The third was nowhere around. He had decided to go out into the world and find his mother, and a great horned owl had seen him. The big bird was having his troubles, too, and had mistaken his prey for a rabbit.

One minute after she'd started for the kennel the next morning, Cary was back in the house. "The deer came close again last night," she said. "They were nibbling on the spreading yews. About four of them, I'd say, from their tracks."

"Evergreen isn't their favorite food. They must be real hungry," Mom decided. "We should put out some hay for them."

"Do we still have wildcats in these parts?"

"Not in years. Why?"

"There's a set of cat tracks leading from the path to the woods. I'll phone Billy later and see if anyone is missing a cat. This was a big one." Then Cary was off to the kennel to feed the pups their first meal of the day.

When she phoned Billy an hour later, the cat expert made the right guess: "Probably a stray."

"But I've never seen a stray cat in our woods," Cary told him.

"That doesn't mean you don't have a few," said Billy. "There's hardly a square mile in America without a stray cat. Some are semiwild and shy away from people. This one is probably hungry. In weather like this, they'll come in close to houses."

Cary planned to enlist the help of Thumper and old Duke in tracking down the stray cat. Then, if they were successful, she intended to leave some food for the stranger.

That plan of action never got underway, for a telephone call from the airport turned Cary's day into a very busy one. The call was from Pop. He had promised to be home by Christmas, and he had kept the promise with several hours to spare. Could Mom pick him up?

She could and she did. But it was a six-hour round trip to the airport, and that meant that Cary remained home alone to feed the pups the rest of their meals and also to feed the adult dogs. In her free moments she fed herself and—as a surprise for her parents—decorated the fir tree that had been standing in the living room for over a week. Christmas Eve had arrived by the time she added the last string of lights to the tree, and just then a car skidded up the long driveway. Her parents were home.

The stray cat was forgotten. Cary wouldn't have had much chance to discuss the subject anyway, for Pop dominated the conversation before, during, and after dinner. The business trip had been a huge success, and he was sure that Big Wind would reward him with a bonus. "If he doesn't," said Pop, "may all the fountain pens leak and be shipped back to him at his expense! Now let's open the presents."

The opening of presents on Christmas Eve rather than Christmas Day was a family tradition, and now the tradition was followed once again. Cary's personal harvest was a bountiful one, from the books to new ski boots to a portable typewriter. She had received all the gifts she'd hoped for. All except one, that is: the kitten. And he was still in her thoughts.

Before falling asleep that night, she reached over and patted Thumper's head. "I'll name him Sleepy," she told the dog, and he grunted as if he understood what she was talking about. "You'll like him. You two will be pals." She was referring to the kitten in her future, of course. For weeks she'd been falling asleep thinking about the kitten, so Sleepy seemed an appropriate name to her.

On this night Cary fell asleep with a contented smile on her face. But she wouldn't have closed her eyes if she'd known what was going to happen on the very next day.

It was seven o'clock on Christmas morning and still dark outdoors. Cary, awake and dressed, was still in her room. She sat on her bed and told Thumper, "The waiting becomes longer each year." The dog opened one eye, closed it, and tried to go back to sleep.

The waiting was for the start of another family tradition: the Christmas stocking. On Christmas morning each member of the family would find a stocking of his own under the tree, and each stocking would be crammed with fruit, nuts, and such small, practical gifts as handkerchiefs, soap, and pencils.

Now Cary could hear her mother moving around downstairs in the living room, and she knew that the waiting was almost over. Mom was probably placing the filled stockings under the tree, but she seemed to be taking a long time. Was something extra being placed under the tree? A little basket or box containing a kitten? A Russian Blue kitten?

Was it possible? Cary closed her eyes and smiled. She was tasting the possibility and finding it reasonable. Perhaps Pop and Mom were better actors than she thought. Had Pop driven over to Billy Hall's during the night and picked up the kitten? She had slept so soundly that she wouldn't have heard the car leaving or returning. It was possible!

Her musing was so pleasant and so deep that she barely heard her Mom's first call from below. But she did distinctly hear the second "Merry Christmas! Come and get it!" She responded by dashing out of her room and racing down the stairs, taking two steps at a time.

Thumper bounded in her wake. All seventy pounds of the yellow Lab banged into Pop as he emerged sleepily from the master bedroom. Pop reached for the door knob, missed it, and sat down hard. He remained where he was until it was safe for him to gain his feet, or until the four Labs who slept in his bedroom—Folly, old Duke, Chub, and the black Moorborn—had scrambled by him and dashed for the tree. "Somebody save the Christmas tree!" Pop shouted. "Here comes the thundering herd!"

He was the last to arrive at the tree and was surprised to find it still standing. The five dogs were sprawled on the rug and looked as innocent as lambs.

"What took you so long?" asked Mom.

"I was ambushed by these beasts," Pop explained. "If there's anything more dangerous than reckless drivers, it must be reckless dogs. Well, let's unload the stockings." He thought it ironic when he found five rawhide bones among his treasures—one for each of the house dogs.

The last gift Cary removed from her stocking was a wristwatch. She knew without being told that it was an expensive one. Still, she had tears in her eyes when she started to thank her parents.

Pop noticed and asked, "What's wrong? Are you unhappy?"

"I'm happy," Cary assured him.

"Then why are you crying?"

"Women like to cry when they're happy and men will never understand," said Mom.

"I'm happy," Cary repeated. "This has been a wonderful Christmas. Golly, this watch must have cost a mint." The girl hoped that she sounded convincing, for she wasn't completely happy. The tears had come because she hadn't really wanted or expected an expensive watch, and there'd been no kitten under the tree. So her parents weren't actors, and they'd planned no great surprise.

"So is it all right with you?" Mom asked, looking at Cary.

"Is what all right?"

"I didn't think you were listening. Now try to concentrate. Big Wind is tossing a gala yuletide brunch for his friends and office slaves today, and your father thinks it would be wise for us to attend. So I thought—if you wouldn't mind staying here and taking care of the animals, and basting the turkey every forty minutes—that we'd attend the brunch and leave early. We'd be back here around five and have Christmas dinner about seven. Do you mind? I'll feed the pups their first two meals."

Cary agreed. At noon on Christmas Day she watched through a kitchen window as the family sedan rolled down the long driveway on the start of the one-hour journey to Big Wind's home.

She wasn't the only one who watched. The pups and the kennel dogs watched from their runs, and a skinny black cat watched from behind a bush at the fringe of the woods. Dangling by the nape of his neck from his mother's jaws was a small, uncomplaining bundle of gray-and-white fur. The bundle was the only surviving kitten of the three who had been born weeks before under the old oak trunk. Kitten number two had died during the night.

Cary didn't see the black cat, and none of the dogs saw her, either. It started to snow, and the hungry queen left the shelter of the bush and pushed through the deep drifts toward the house. She disliked dogs and she didn't trust people, but she had to find food on this day or her baby wouldn't see another. Instinct may have told her that the risk was worth the effort.

Cary sensed that something out of the ordinary was happening. Always, when she mixed dog food in the kitchen, she could count on an audience of five house dogs. They would sit as close to her as possible, with their heads cocked and eyes alert and tails thumping the floor, watching her every move as she went back and forth between table and counter. The puppies' third meal of the day was being prepared, but the big dogs didn't mind watching. Some of the food might spill to the floor.

Cary moved around the dogs and went to the stove for the soft-boiled eggs. The dogs looked at each other rather than at her. Then four stood as one and walked single file into the hallway that led to the living room. Only Folly remained. She was always hungry, and a team of wild horses would have had trouble dragging her from the presence of food.

So Folly was the only dog remaining when Cary turned away from the stove on her way back to the counter with the pot of eggs. What had proved more attractive than food to the others? It had to be something, and Cary was curious.

She placed the pot on the counter, then hurried down the hallway to the living room. The sight that greeted her brought her to a sudden halt. There were two dogs at each of the tall, narrow windows on either side of the solid front door. Old Duke and his son Thumper shared the left window, while Chub and Moorborn looked out of the right window. All four were standing on their rear legs and resting their forepaws on the window sills. All four heads were up, all ears forward, and all tails stiff as pokers.

Obviously, they were watching something on the roofed front terrace. Whatever it was, the dogs didn't consider it dangerous or they would have been growling and barking and trying to scratch their way through the door.

Cary walked slowly to the left window and looked out over the heads of Thumper and his sire. Thumper whined anxiously as she approached, but neither he nor the others turned their heads.

At first Cary didn't see what the dogs saw, for the stone terrace faced eastward and was already bathed

in shadows. Then she did see the object of their
attention: a big, skinny black cat.

The cat was crouched smack in the middle of the
terrace. She looked ready to spring in any direction,
and her only discernible movements were in her
eyes and tail. As her eyes moved slowly from one
window to the other, just the tip of her otherwise
straight, still tail waved in the opposite direction.
She lifted her head, opened her mouth, and cried
out to her audience.

It was a loud, complaining cry, and it sounded
faint and weak on the other side of the door. But
Cary heard it. "That cat is all skin and bones,"
Cary advised the dogs. "Stay here and keep an eye
on her while I find some food. She looks starved."

She hurried to the kitchen and prepared a bowl
of lukewarm milk. "What else does a cat like to
eat?" she asked Folly, who was still there keeping
her eyes on the puppy food. A handful of chopped
beef meat for the pups went into the bowl, and
then a shredded crust of bread. That was all the
bowl would hold.

The black cat scooted to the far end of the terrace as Cary opened the front door. There she
stopped and watched as Cary placed the bowl down,
then turned and went back into the house, closing
the door behind her.

Cary and the Labs looked through the windows.
It seemed like a full minute to Cary, but it was just
a few seconds before the black stranger started for
the bowl of food. It did take a couple of minutes,

however, before the cat reached the bowl. Every few feet, the hungry queen would stop, look carefully in all directions, and then take a few more steps forward before stopping and looking again. Her need for food was desperate, but she was in unfamiliar territory and alert for any danger. When she reached the bowl she showed restraint and caution: long looks to her right, her left, her rear, and to both windows. Only then did she extend her head over the bowl and dip her tongue into the milk. At first she lapped in a tentative fashion, but within seconds she stepped up the tempo and was dining in a hurried, almost greedy way.

The bowl was still half full when the cat backed off, turned, and ran across the terrace. She jumped down the steps and out of sight of Cary and the dogs.

"Now what frightened her?" asked Cary of the dogs. "I didn't hear anything. Well, she didn't eat much. Maybe she'll come back later. We'll leave the food and hope it doesn't freeze. Come on. The show's over." The dogs looked at her. "I know, I know, maybe I should have invited her in, but you don't know Pop as well as I do."

The dogs dropped to all fours and followed her back to the kitchen, and she was unaware that Thumper didn't go all the way. Once in the hallway, he turned and trotted back to the window and reclaimed his viewing position. It was as if he wasn't willing to believe that the show was over, and he was right. Within a few minutes the yellow

Lab became the only witness to see the return of the black cat.

She didn't return alone. This time she was carrying her gray-and-white kitten, and she dropped him right next to the bowl. When he didn't move, she tried to nudge his head over the rim of the bowl, but she was not successful. Four inches was nothing to the cat, but it was a solid barrier to her cold, weak baby. So she picked him up and dumped him into the bowl.

The watching Thumper emitted a single, loud bark. The sound set off all sorts of action!

The black cat heard him. The bark meant danger to her. She backed off a few steps, then crouched and arched her back, her tail shooting skyward.

The four dogs in the kitchen heard the bark. They came charging down the hallway and into the living room, all yapping in full voice. And Cary came running right behind, shouting to them to be quiet. But they couldn't hear her. Indeed, she could hardly hear her own shouts.

The noise inside the house frightened the black cat. She retreated to the far end of the terrace, then remembered her baby in the bowl. As she started back to rescue him, the door opened and dogs seemed to pour from the house, followed by a girl.

The black cat turned and ran. She never saw what happened when the dogs discovered her kitten.

Thumper was first out the door and first to the bowl. He poked the kitten with his nose, as if

wondering what the small thing could be. The kitten, drenched in milk, didn't smell anything like a cat to the dog.

Seconds later, Moorborn and Folly were at the bowl licking the kitten. Folly's concern was short-lived. Her tongue tasted beef-flavored milk, and she tried to push the baby aside and get at the unexpected meal.

Cary arrived and pushed her hand down between the dogs' heads. She scooped up the wet, cold newcomer and carried him into the house. She didn't know if the little kitten was alive or dead, but she thought she knew what she must do: just what she would have done if the wet, cold bundle of fur in her hands had been a puppy. She grabbed a towel and rubbed the small body, briskly but gently, until the coat was dry. That brought warmth to the body and helped the blood to circulate.

Her patient remained motionless as she wrapped him in a dry towel and placed him on the kitchen table. Only his head stuck out of the towel. His eyes were closed.

Cary stepped to the telephone and dialed Billy Hall's number. She needed advice, and she hoped she'd find Billy at home. When she heard him say hello she uttered a long sigh of relief and then proceeded to pour out the story of how she had found the kitten, and of what she had done to try and save him. She spoke rapidly, so rapidly that Billy grasped only part of what she said. "So what do I do now?" she pleaded.

"But is the kitten still alive?"

"I think so, I hope so. . . . Wait!"

"Wait for what?" asked Billy.

"I think his head just moved. Yes, again! And now he seems to be yawning, but his eyes are still closed."

"Keep him warm and we'll be right there," said Billy. "Oh, and you might heat some milk. Half milk, half water. Be seeing you."

She heard the click on his end and put down the phone, constantly keeping her eyes on the kitten. "The experts are coming," she said to the kitten. "Just stay warm and calm and you'll be safe." As if in reply, the kitten opened one eye and voiced a single, faint meow.

A chorus of muffled barks reached the room. The dogs were complaining outside the back door, reminding Cary that she'd shut them out of the house when she closed the front door. She opened the back door for them.

The snow had stopped falling. On the limb of a tree that stood about thirty feet from the front terrace, the black cat worked her way back to the trunk. From her vantage point above the ground, the skinny queen had seen Cary rescue the kitten and carry him into the house. She'd seen the door shut and watched the dogs as they waited on the terrace and finally trotted down the steps, around the house, and out of her sight.

And as the dogs barked at the back door, she was jumping to a lower limb, and then a lower one, and finally to a bank of snow. From there she headed through the snow to the woods—never pausing, never looking back, as if she knew that this one baby of hers was in safe hands. There would be other babies in her own future, and hopefully they would be born in warmer seasons of the year.

No one at Walden—none of the people and none of the dogs—ever saw the black cat again.

Cary had just placed the pan of water and milk on the stove when the Hall's car pulled into the driveway at Walden. Mrs. Hall was at the wheel and Cary wasn't sure how the woman would react to a pack of dogs. She herded the Labs into the hallway, told them to be quiet, and shut the door. Moments later she opened the back door for Billy and his mother. And for a while she felt like the most useless human on earth. Billy and his mother were too preoccupied to waste many words on her.

"Just as I suspected," said Mrs. Hall as she examined the kitten. "This poor darling hasn't had more than a morsel of food in ten days. Emaciated. Is the milk ready?"

"Almost warm enough," replied Billy, who had tested it with one finger.

"Not too warm. Just above room temperature."

"I know," said Billy. "Cary, you have a five-day supply of milk here. I'll need a cup and saucer. And a spoon."

For the next few minutes no one said a word. As soon as the milk was warm enough, Billy poured out half a cup and brought it to his mother. She held the kitten on her lap and offered him a spoonful of the liquid, but he turned his head away. The little gray and white had received milk only from his mother's nipple, and the spoon didn't interest him.

Mrs. Hall knew what to do with a reluctant kitten. She dipped one finger in the diluted milk, then gently opened the kitten's jaws and inserted her wet finger. That gave the little one a taste of the milk, and his tongue found a stronger taste when he tried to lick away the milk the woman dabbed on his nose. Next came step number three: the kitten was placed on the table and held upright while Billy pushed the small head down to the milk in the saucer. The little patient sniffed the milk, then started lapping away with his tongue.

As they watched him satisfy at least part of his appetite, Mrs. Hall turned to Cary and asked, "Now just how did you find him? Billy wasn't quite sure about what you told him over the phone."

Cary told the story as she had lived it a half-hour before. There wasn't much to tell about the black cat, except that she looked starved. And there was less to tell about the kitten, for she had found him in the bowl and could only assume that the big cat had brought him there.

When she finished, Billy spoke up. "Do you want to keep this kitten?"

"Of course."

"But what about your father?"

"I thought I might trick him," Cary confessed. "You see, Duke is his favorite dog. In Pop's eyes, Duke can do no wrong. And Duke is always bringing home something that he found in the woods. So it seems to me that if Duke found this starving kitten in the woods and decided to save his life by bringing him home, why Pop might change his mind about cats, or at least about this particular kitten. What do you think?"

"Certainly worth a try," agreed Billy.

"It won't do!" said Mrs. Hall. "Honesty is always best, and Cary doesn't have the sort of face that can tell a convincing lie, anyway. No, my dear, tell the story exactly as it happened. If your father has an ounce of sentiment in him, he will find a special meaning in this happening. More than just accidental fate is involved. After all, this is Christmas! Well, I have kittens to feed at home. You stay here, Billy, and advise Cary about kitten diet and care. I'll send your father in an hour or so."

Cary told her not to bother. "My parents will be home soon, and one of them will drive Billy home. Thanks for coming."

"You have a very lovely kitten," said Mrs. Hall. She was just about to go out the door when she sniffed and asked, "Is something burning?"

"Golly!'" cried Cary. "I forgot to baste the turkey!" And as she rushed for the oven she added, "And I forgot to feed the puppies, too!"

3

SLEEPY

WITHIN the hour, Cary was telling the story about the kitten for the third time that day. Her audience consisted of her parents, Billy, five Labradors, and the kitten, although the kitten was sound asleep on Billy's lap.

There was one small variation in the third telling. Cary had old Duke playing the hero's role. She said that Duke had discovered the kitten on the terrace and that Duke had been the first to lick the little fellow. Billy knew that hadn't been the case, and her Mom knew just from looking at her face that it wasn't so, but Pop believed her. He'd been watching Duke and patting the dog.

"Always knew you had a soft heart," Pop said to

the dog. "You're the humanitarian in the family."

"And you didn't see the mother cat again?" Mom asked. "Did you look for her?"

"About an hour ago," Cary explained. "We took Thumper and Duke along, and we found her tracks, but we lost them in the woods."

"As a matter of fact, we found another set of tracks in the woods," Billy said. "So I'd say you have at least two strays out there. Duke found the second set." Billy had really found those tracks himself, but he was willing to flatter Duke for the kitten's sake.

"Finest marking dog I've ever owned," Pop told the young man. "I'll take you duck hunting sometime and show you what I mean. But two stray cats? I've never seen a single cat in our woods."

"There are strays all over America, sir," Billy assured him. "According to the authorities, there are over ten million strays in this country."

"Really?" asked Pop. "Then that explains why Bob Echelson hasn't returned home."

"Bob who?" questioned Cary, taking the bait.

"A friend of mine who started walking from New York City to Kansas City. He left last June, and along the way he was going to count the stray cats. I guess he's still walking and counting." He laughed uproariously, but he laughed alone. The dogs didn't even wag their tails, and old Duke merely yawned.

"There's nothing funny about ten million homeless cats," Mom reminded her husband after he had enjoyed his joke. "Now what do you think about this poor kitten?"

Pop scratched his head and gazed at the ceiling. He was thinking, and Cary thought he would never stop. The kitten's fate was in Pop's hands, and now was the critical moment. Would she be permitted to keep the kitten?

Finally, Pop said, "You asked me what I think about this kitten? Why, I think he's cute, but aren't all kittens cute?"

"You are avoiding the issue," Mom advised him.

"That's true, very true. I don't like to make a hasty decision, because most of the hasty ones I've made in my life have caused regret later on. However these circumstances are unusual, and so is the timing. For those reasons, and despite my well-known objections to the cat family, I think we can give this kitten a home here. But on trial, mind you! Only on trial! If he ever becomes a nuisance, out the window he must go. Agreed?"

It was a moment for celebration at Walden. The kitten had found a home, a mistress, and a future. Cary shouted, planted a kiss on the kitten's head, hugged her father, hugged her mother, and finally hugged Billy. Then, still shouting, she raced down the hallway and around the living room. The dogs bounded after her, barking their joy. They didn't know why she was so happy, but whatever the reason, she had their support.

Back in the kitchen, Billy was explaining that the girl's new pet was a purebred, or an American

Shorthair, even though she would never have registration papers to prove it. "People who don't know better would call him a mongrel or an alley cat, but they'd be wrong. He's just as purebred as your Labrador Retrievers."

"What I like most about him is his broad head," said Mom. "Just like a Lab's."

"Yes," agreed Pop, "he does have a broad head for his size. Well, at least he has one virtue going for him."

The celebration continued on through the dinner hour, and the conversation—for the first time in years—revolved around cats rather than dogs. One good reason was the presence of the kitten, of course, but a stronger one was the presence of Billy. The cat expert had been happy to accept a dinner invitation, despite the fact that he'd already enjoyed one Christmas dinner with his own family.

The only times the talk swerved from cats was when Billy was eating. At all other times he spouted information that he thought might be helpful in raising the kitten. "Offering milk and meat to the mother cat was proper," he said to Cary, "but you were wrong to include the bread crusts."

"Bread is the staff of life," said Pop.

"Not for a cat," Billy replied. "You see, sir, the cat's digestive tract is different from any other animal's, including ours. He has a hard time digesting

starchy foods. Another food to avoid is raw pork. Leads to trichinosis, a serious disease. Otherwise, it's safe for a cat to eat almost anything, raw or cooked."

"If bread isn't the staff of life for a cat, then milk is," announced Pop.

"No, sir!" said Billy, and Cary and her parents waited while he munched and swallowed a bit of turkey dressing before continuing. "At any time during his growing period, or perhaps after he becomes an adult, he may turn his nose up at milk. But what he'll always need is fresh water. I've forgotten the exact percentages, but well over sixty percent of his body weight is water, and his organs can't function properly without water."

"If water is so important to them, then cats should be better swimmers," Pop chuckled.

"Cats make fine swimmers, sir, but some like to swim and some don't, just like people."

"You know something, Billy?" asked Pop. "The more you talk, the more ignorant I become. My wife and daughter will lose all respect for me. I refuse to say anything more."

Billy looked embarrassed, but Mom rushed to the rescue. "How much milk does the kitten get at each feeding?"

"I wrote it down, but he can always have more," explained Billy. "Don't worry. A kitten isn't like a puppy. A kitten seldom overeats. He'll know when to quit."

Pop opened his mouth to defend the intelligence

of all puppies. But he remembered his pledge and didn't say a word. The boy was probably right, he thought, and it was proper thinking.

Actually, Pop managed to stay off the subject of cats for another hour, or until he was driving Billy home. Then, as they approached Billy's house, he asked, "What is your honest opinion of Blockhead, Billy?"

"Of whom?"

"Blockhead. Cary's kitten. Great name, don't you think? He has the broad, blocky head of a Lab."

"The name fits, sir, but he already has a name. Didn't your daughter tell you? She's already named him Sleepy. Quite appropriate, too, I think. The poor little fellow will do more sleeping than eating for the next few weeks. He's in pretty bad shape."

"Will he live?"

"Don't worry about that, sir. The recuperative powers of a cat are amazing. Where there's life, there's a lot more than hope. But just to be on the safe side, your wife is taking Sleepy to the vet tomorrow. That's my house on the right, sir." The boy waited for the car to slow and stop before adding, "Will you come in for a few minutes? My mother would love to show you her cats."

"Some other time, Billy. Tomorrow is a workday for me."

"Oh, yes, I forgot. Thanks for the lift home. Goodnight, sir." The boy opened the car door, paused, then closed the door. "I'd just like to say that I admire the way you've taken all this in stride, sir. You've made me change my mind about you. I had thought that you were a contradictory American, but you're not."

"I'm not?"

"No. You have revealed yourself as a true American and a believer in democracy, a system of government where the majority opinion shall prevail."

"I appreciate the compliment," said Pop, "although I'm not sure that I understand."

"In the United States," explained Billy, "there are about twelve million more pet cats than dogs. So it follows that there must be more cat lovers than dog lovers. We are in the majority, so to speak, and now you have joined the ranks. Goodnight, and thanks again."

"Goodnight," said Pop, and Billy departed so quickly that there was no time to say more. Pop chuckled as he turned the car around and headed for home. He liked Billy, and thought of him as the only amusing, entertaining young man in Cary's life. Then, as he recalled all that the boy had just said, Pop laughed outright. It wasn't likely that he, a lifelong disliker of cats, would change his mind because of a single skinny kitten, even if the kitten did have a broad head. Still, he hoped for his daughter's sake that the kitten would behave himself. It was worth the try.

Back in his own home, he found his family sitting by the fireplace rehashing the day's events. The house dogs were sprawled on the floor watching the flames in the fireplace. Each dog rested his head on a portion of another dog. It was a peaceful scene, and none of them—wife, daughter, or dogs—stirred as the head of the house crossed the room and announced, "I have returned!" To his wife's question about what took him so long, he replied, "I wasn't engaged in any Communist activity, I can tell you that. I am a true American, or a cat lover, according to Billy." He sat down, looked around and asked, "Where's Blockhead? I mean, where's the kitten? Sleepy?"

"Asleep on his own bed," Cary told him. "Come on, I'll show you." She led her father into the kitchen and through to the adjacent laundry room. There, in one corner of the room and away from any drafts, Cary and Billy had fashioned a bed for the kitten. It was a small cardboard carton, with the top flaps removed and a hole cut in one end. The bottom was lined with newspapers for insulation, and on top of the papers were shredded old rags. Sleepy had huddled himself into the rags and was sound asleep.

A foot from the opening to his box was a shallow bowl of water. And two feet from that was a sawdust-filled metal tray. Pop pointed to it. "I see he has his own bathroom facilities."

There was an undertone of pride in her voice as Cary nodded and said, "Yes, and he's already used it once of his own accord. We placed him there after the first two feedings, but nobody had to tell him where to go the third time. We think he's already housebroken. Want to bet?"

"No thanks," said Pop. "Cats seem to be smarter

than I'd been led to believe. Think he'll wander during the night?"

"Want to bet?"

Pop shook his head no, and they returned to the living room and the fire.

About twenty minutes later, after Cary had retired, her parents decided to do the same. But both of them were restless, and sleep didn't come immediately to either of them.

"Are you thinking about the kitten?" asked Mom.

"I am. Do you think he's safe enough and warm enough?"

"Well, he survived sleeping in a colder place, and why shouldn't he be safe? Still. . . ."

"Yes?" asked Pop. "Still what?"

"Cary told me that the kitten made this the happiest Christmas of her life. Do you know what would make it just perfect for her? Why don't we let the kitten sleep in her room? Can't you just see her face, and Thumper's expression, when they awaken in the morning and find Sleepy in the room? What do you say?" asked Mom as she climbed out of bed.

"You're on your way, so what can I say?" said Pop. "Except, if it's going to be a surprise, try not to awaken Cary."

But Cary was still awake when Mom carried the kitten in his box into her room. "What's up?" asked the girl.

"We decided that Sleepy's bed should be in here with you," said Mom. "Put on the light."

The sleeping box went into the closet, where it would be safe from drafts, and the closet door was left ajar. Sleepy didn't awaken, but when the light went out and Mom left the room, the little gray and white was purring in his sleep, as if in appreciation.

"Where was Thumper?" asked Pop when his wife returned to their room. "On Cary's bed?"

"He was sleeping on the floor at the foot of her bed, of course. You know better than to ask that question," said Mom. "Why, he's a well-trained dog. He hasn't slept on her bed since he was a puppy."

She was right, but only at that particular moment. Minutes later, when Thumper was sure that Cary was asleep, the dog leaped onto her bed. He curled on top of the blankets, but the new comfort didn't seem to satisfy him.

The big dog stirred, jumped to the floor, and walked to the closet. He nudged open the door, then stuck his head down into the kitten's box and gently lifted Sleepy in his jaws.

The kitten didn't complain as Thumper carried him to the bed and placed him on the blankets. And he purred as the dog again jumped onto the bed and nuzzled him close. If Mom had paid a return visit and turned on the light, she would have found Cary curled up and sleeping under the covers, and Thumper on top of the covers, curled up and sleeping back-to-back with Cary. And she would have seen a gray-and-white ball huddled between Thumper's legs and against his belly.

The only one still awake in the house was Pop. A disturbing thought had crossed his mind: what if, on next Christmas, a black mare trotted out of the woods and placed a hungry colt on the doorstep?

Thus Sleepy came to Walden and found a home there. And just as Billy had predicted, his presence didn't cause a ripple of excitement in the house. The big dogs recognized him for what he was: a baby. They didn't chase him, they were careful to avoid stepping on him, and they weren't offended when he tried to play with their wagging tails. True, four were unhappy and growled a bit when he was big enough to stick his head into their dinner plates. Only Thumper didn't seem to mind. He gulped down a meal in such rapid fashion that the kitten had time to steal no more than crumbs.

The peace would have been broken if Sleepy had ever visited the puppies. Ten weeks old, they didn't know their own strength and would have trampled him in their rough-and-tumble play. Fortunately, Sleepy never did get loose among that particular litter of Walden pups. All had been sold and each went to his new home right after the holidays. The kitten would be bigger and better able to handle himself by the time a new litter of pups arrived.

Every so often Pop forgot and called him Blockhead, but neither the kitten nor Cary seemed to mind. "I'm sorry," Pop would apologize, "but his head seems to be about one-half of his total body. He may become a freak."

"Don't worry," Cary told him. "Kittens are like pups. They don't mature in balance. Sleepy's other parts will catch up with his head, sooner or later. Would you like to hear what Billy says?"

"Yes. What does Sleepy's lawyer have to say?"

"He says that the big head means that Sleepy will grow into a bigger-than-average cat. The average adult male is six to seven pounds, but Sleepy will end up at ten to twelve."

"What does the lawyer say about the colors? There seems to be less white up front."

"The balance between gray and white will remain constant from now on."

It was Billy's prediction, not hers, and it was one of the rare mistakes about cats that he ever made. In the next few weeks Sleepy's gray tail began sporting some white hairs, and then more white hairs appeared. The end result was an inch of white on the tip of his tail, as if he'd dipped his tail in paint.

Otherwise, he was solid tones of gray to his very front. The stockings on his forelegs remained white, and so did the bib that covered his chest and ran down to his belly. And the white over his nose and forehead remained, giving him the appearance of a bandit wearing a mask. Amber eyes peered through the mask.

Thus except for the tip of his tail and a gradual darkening of his gray parts, the colors Sleepy wore in January were the ones he wore for the rest of his life. And in the next eight months he packed on all the weight he'd ever carry living up to Billy's other prediction: a dozen pounds. Cary thought this was quite an achievement for somebody who'd entered the world at no more than four ounces.

Although he didn't reach his full length in that first winter of his life, he was growing rapidly and learning all sorts of wonderful things about himself. While the dogs were giants compared to him, he could twist and turn and move more quickly than any of them. When he jumped playfully for Chub's tail, the Lab would lunge for him, but he would turn and scoot under her and away before her head was close. Like all his cat cousins in the world, Sleepy's coordination of muscles and bones made him almost unbelievably agile. He could see better than the dogs, too, and could run circles around them in a dark room, although he was as helpless as they in total darkness.

As for his manners, he never betrayed Cary's confidence that he knew where to go when Nature called. No matter where he was or what he was doing in the house, he'd jump up and dash for his sanitary pan. Sometimes this meant running under dogs and around people, but Sleepy always managed to reach his destination in time. In that respect, he was the perfect cat.

Mom and Cary agreed that a kitten was far less

trouble in the house than a puppy, if Sleepy was any example. He didn't chew expensive slippers into shreds, or bite through chair legs, or even knock over standing lamps and wastebaskets. When they mentioned these virtues to Pop, hoping to impress him, he shrugged and replied: "Maybe kittens are too dumb to be destructive. He's never going to learn to stay off the furniture. What is this, March? So he's over three months old and I still find him sleeping on my favorite chair every night. Why, a month-old pup knows better than that!"

"Duke is ten and he still sleeps in your chair," Cary reminded him.

"Yes, but he has the brains and the courtesy to jump off the chair when I enter the room," said Pop. "Sleepy just looks at me and doesn't budge."

As far as the head of the house was concerned, Sleepy was still on trial, still expendable. To his surprise, the kitten hadn't developed into a real nuisance, and at times he found himself enjoying the presence of the growing gray and white. Indeed, one time he found himself bragging about the newcomer, something that he'd never dreamed he'd do about any member of the cat family. It happened when he was lunching with other slaves from Big Wind's office, and the conversation turned to pets. He was able to tell how Sleepy was riding Thumper and sometimes managed to stay on top of the dog for ten feet before falling. They didn't believe him, but it was the truth—as Mom, Cary, Billy, and others could testify. How Sleepy had learned to become a jockey was something nobody would ever know. He and the dog had somehow worked it out together.

On the day the four persons witnessed Sleepy stay aboard Thumper for more than forty feet, Billy couldn't refrain from boasting, "This proves the cat is smarter than the dog! Who ever heard of a dog inventing a means of transportation?"

"You're forgetting the Otter Hound," Pop reminded him. "The breed got its name because these dogs can cross a river without getting their feet wet. They stand on top of an otter!"

Until Cary laughed, Billy almost believed him.

"When are you going to make the great announcement?" asked Mom on the last Sunday in March. Pop looked puzzled, so she continued. "I refer to Sleepy's trial period with us. Isn't it about time to admit that he's been a great success? Cary's still wondering if he's going to be a permanent member of the family. So?"

"Too early for a final judgment," Pop declared. "I admit that the creature has impressed me, but I'm waiting for the snow to disappear. I want to see how he conducts himself outdoors."

"The songbirds?"

"Yes! I hope he doesn't, but if this cat kills a single. . . ."

"Oh, for heaven's sake," Mom interrupted. "A

bird that is foolish enough to be caught by a cat doesn't have brains enough to survive anyway! Furthermore, most cats don't even bother birds. Scientific research has proven over and over that the diet of a cat left to his own devices is mostly rodent, then insect, and finally—or about five percent—bird!"

"You're not talking like a life member of the Audubon Society, you are talking like that young lawyer, Billy Hall!"

"Of course. He does all the research for Cary, and she informs me. Anything wrong with that?"

Pop took his time and lit his pipe before answering. "No, and I think I might as well use this source of information to my own advantage. Would you please ask Cary to ask Billy about Sleepy's purrs? I don't know if you've noticed, but he seems to have a variety of purrs. At least ten. It seems to me that each purr must have its own meaning, and I'm wondering if each purr is a different degree of his disapproval of me."

"A cat only purrs when he's content."

"Yes, but this one may find contentment in disliking me. When those amber eyes turn into slits and his tail doesn't wave, I sometimes feel like a robin."

"Suppose we make the last day in April the day of your great decision about Sleepy?" asked Mom. "He'll have been outdoors for several weeks by then. Agreed?"

Pop sort of nodded, but it wasn't anything definite. And Mom didn't repeat the question. She knew better than to press him, and she was quite sure that Sleepy was winning the battle for her husband's favor. He was bragging about Sleepy at the office, wasn't he? And he was wondering if purrs could be translated, wasn't he?

The life member of the Audubon Society, wife, mother, dog fancier, and kitten lover was a patient woman. April 30th was only five weeks away. She could wait for the great decision.

But the decision came before that, and it was based on something that caused her to shudder every time she remembered.

4

PERILS OF YOUTH

APRIL Fool's Day passed quietly at Walden. No one tried to play tricks on anyone else, but all were fooled anyway. The fooler was the weather.

It was a bright, sunny day, so warm that everybody said it was just like spring and wouldn't it be nice if it lasted? Everybody knew, of course, that it wouldn't last. There would be at least two or three more snowstorms before true spring arrived.

But they were fooled. True spring had really arrived, as promised by the calendar. Within the week there were only traces of snow in the woods, and patches of grass started showing on the lawns. Pop ordered the garden seeds he'd meant to order in January, robins crowded bluejays off the feeders, and Cary began worrying about the final exams that were still two months away.

For Sleepy, the melting snow and clear warm days meant more time spent outdoors. There were all sorts of new things for him to discover and investigate, and it wasn't long before he found a special place to visit every day: the old stone wall that separated the upper lawn from the woods. He had his choice of any number of flat rocks atop the wall, and one was as good as another for sunning himself and waiting.

Although he was a model of stillness, birds, chipmunks, rabbits, squirrels, and field mice were all aware of his presence because he was out in the open. They kept a safe distance from him. The one exception was a blundering, fat toad who lived in the wall under one of the kitten's favorite rocks. The toad couldn't see anything until it moved, and he was too slow to escape whenever the gray-and-white creature materialized out of nowhere and rushed for him. But the toad's life was never in danger. Sleepy was always careful to retract his claws before pawing at the toad and rolling him over. The kitten would play with him for a while and then permit him to go his own way.

At that stage of his life Sleepy would have done the same with a chipmunk or a rabbit or anything else. Hunting was only a game to him. He was too well-fed to kill.

He could usually count on another sort of adventure at least once a day, when Cary returned from school and made sure the dogs had sufficient exercise. She enjoyed leading the dogs on a journey to the high boulders that crested a cliff. It was a half-mile journey, all uphill, and the kitten would tag along until he tired. When that happened, he'd drop out and wait for the others to return.

If they took too long, Sleepy would do some exploring on his own. Usually this meant trying to find a certain outcropping of rocks, almost hidden by the rotting trunks of fallen trees. There was a little cave between two of the rocks, and the kitten was curious about who lived in that cave. He'd sit off about ten feet and watch the entrance.

It was an ideal waiting place, for it was within hearing distance of both the path to the cliff and a second path that Cary and the dogs sometimes used when returning through the woods.

In other years and seasons the cave had been home to a variety of owners: mice, insects, a red fox, and snakes. Now, in this first spring of Sleepy's life, it was the stormy-weather shelter of a huge orange tomcat. He was an old fellow, a stray who had lived a lonesome life for more than a dozen years and had survived at least one severe winter. Both of his ears were rounded at the tips, sure signs that they'd been frozen. A huge chunk was missing from his right ear, evidence of a long-ago cat fight. His tail was a thick four-inch stub—a farmer's son had found him feasting in a pigeon loft and shot off the rest.

The battle-scarred veteran considered himself the

king of Walden woods. He had been around for months, and it was his tracks that Cary and Billy had discovered on Christmas Day. The dogs were aware that the cat was around, for they'd scented him many times. They had searched for him and never found him. And they had no way, of course, to tell the news to their people or to Sleepy.

The kitten knew somebody lived in the cave. His nose told him that much. And while he was as curious as any other kitten in the world, he seemed content to wait for the cave's owner to announce himself. Something held him back from entering the cave. It was as if he sensed danger but still wanted to tempt it.

The long-delayed meeting between the dogs, the tomcat, and the kitten took place on the second Tuesday in April.

It was midafternoon and the house dogs had been fed. Old Duke and Thumper couldn't wait for Cary to come home from school. They may have had a quick swim in mind or perhaps they remembered the porcupine Cary hadn't permitted them to pursue the day before.

They trotted across the upper lawn and through the opening in the old stone wall. Sleepy heard them coming, then saw them. He jumped off the wall and voiced a catcall that meant wait for me.

The dogs probably heard him, but they didn't wait. They trotted along the path through the woods, and Sleepy paced as fast as he could, trying to catch up with them. He complained as he moved along, but his plaintive meows didn't slow down the dogs.

Thumper and Duke were out of the kitten's sight after the first minute. Sleepy increased his speed until he was galloping along in rabbitlike manner, but he didn't close the gap between them. Finally, he stopped and rested.

He wasn't far from the hidden cave, and that's where he headed when he felt refreshed. The kitten wasn't in any hurry. He walked along through a grove of old white pines, not making a sound, thanks to the thick layer of dead pine needles on the ground.

Suddenly he stopped. He'd heard a strange sound. Sleepy was capable of making that sound himself, but he never had, for the occasion for using it had never occurred in his young life.

The kitten turned his head to the right, trying to find the source of the sound. It had been a hiss, really, and now he heard it again and was able to locate the hisser.

The big orange tomcat stood just off a straight line to the cave. The orange was only a shade of gray to Sleepy, of course, since cats are just as color blind as most other animals. And the tomcat must have seemed an alien creature to the kitten. In all his life, the only cat he'd really known was his own mother, and chances were slim that he remembered her. So he had enjoyed only canine society until this moment, and probably considered himself to be a dog.

The veteran stray hissed a third warning. Any other cat on earth would have realized what he was saying: This is my kingdom, and visiting cats are not welcome. So beat it, or get ready to fight for your life.

But to Sleepy, the hiss was just the strange sound repeated once again. The curious kitten started to walk toward the tomcat, purring friendly greetings as he advanced. And the orange tomcat, who had fully expected the kitten to run, arched his back, shot the stump of his tail skyward, and growled.

This new, unpleasant sound brought Sleepy to an abrupt halt. He stared, backed up a few steps, then arched his own back. Sudden fright told him not to trust the big creature. And then, as the orange warrior stepped slowly toward him, the kitten growled. The discovery that he could also manufacture the sound pleased him. He made the sound again, and it wasn't misinterpreted by the tomcat.

The experienced tom started purring in a most friendly fashion. He came within three feet of the kitten before turning and walking away. It was an act of deception, and it worked!

Sleepy relaxed. The big cat's purrs lulled him into a false sense of security. He hurried to the orange tom's side, rubbed against one of his thick forelegs and voiced peaceful purrs.

It was an act of friendship, but it set off a fire. The orange cat reared, twisted, snarled, and came down on Sleepy with all his front claws extended.

Sleepy's eyes were his intended targets and there was nothing wrong with his aim. But the youngster's reflexes were sharper than the veteran's, and the sudden move and the snarl had warned him that something was amiss. The kitten twisted and dove under his assailant, and the descending claws dug into the bed of dead pine needles.

The unharmed, frightened Sleepy didn't wait for a second try at friendship. He raced through the pine grove at a speed he'd never attained before, and the furious tomcat kept close to his tail. Every twenty feet or so the big orange would scream his rage, and every scream encouraged the kitten to fly over the ground a little faster.

At the very edge of the grove loomed a two-foot rock. Sleepy used it as a springboard to leap for the trunk of a fat yellow birch. Using his claws for holding agents, he scampered up the trunk.

The old tomcat stopped and sat down at the base of the trunk. He looked up and watched the climbing Sleepy. He knew that the kitten was fleeing to nowhere, for the trunk was branchless—it had snapped off in some previous winter's storm. Sleepy could climb no more than fifteen feet.

When Sleepy reached that altitude he found himself alone on a rough, splintered perch. Staying put was the only safe thing to do, and that's what he did. He had only two other alternatives: to descend and risk being torn apart; or to leap for the nearest branch of a pine tree, a distance of twenty feet. He didn't give the leap a second thought. All members of the cat family are excellent judges of distance, and a glance told the kitten that he'd never make the closest branch.

Things were stalemated for several minutes, until the winded tomcat felt fresh enough to renew his attack. He strolled to the birch trunk, leaped, and started his climb. From up above, Sleepy watched him come. His whole body trembled. He was in a crouch and didn't dare arch his back for fear of tumbling off his uneven perch.

The orange stray dug his front claws into the birch trunk just inches below the break. He couldn't quite reach the kitten with his teeth, but he stretched his neck and made a vain attempt at biting the kitten anyway. It was a mistake. Sleepy reacted by batting away with his right paw and raking the attacker's nose with his unsheathed claws.

The damage wasn't serious, and the old tom's shriek was one of slight pain mixed with surprise. He withdrew his head and moved down the trunk a few inches before uttering a cry that sent chills up Sleepy's spine. The cry was really an undulating scream, the blood-curdling one that toms reserve for each other when they are about to fight for a queen cat's favors. It's a familiar sound all over the world, or wherever there are queen cats, tomcats, and backyard fences and full moons.

He screamed a second time, as if to make sure that Sleepy heard him, then moved up the trunk and over the top. He was rushing Sleepy's perch, sure that he'd either destroy the kitten or push him off. There wasn't enough room for both of them.

The big tom was still pulling his front over the top when Sleepy jumped. He went almost straight up, twisted, and came down hind legs first on the big cat's back. The kitten groped frantically until his front paws found holding places over the orange warrior's shoulders. In a rather accidental manner, Sleepy had found at least momentary safety. He was safe so long as the tomcat clung to the tree, or until they both tumbled to the ground.

Their acrobatics had been watched from below by a silent audience of two: Duke and Thumper. On their return trip from the cliff, the two dogs had heard some strange, high-pitched cries, and they'd detoured to investigate.

Now the two dogs were sitting side by side some twenty feet from the base of the yellow birch, and they were looking up and watching the antics of the kitten and the cat. At the moment there was nothing that they could do to help Sleepy. They were ready for action, but they were not high jumpers.

Neither the old cat nor the young one knew that the dogs were below. Like a fireman carrying a child on his back, the big stray descended very slowly, inching one leg down and then another, making sure he had a firm hold with the first before moving the second. He had learned what most cats must learn: a cat's claws are perfectly designed for climbing, but since none are reversed they are all wrong for upside-down traveling.

The slow, orderly descent ended six feet from the ground. The tomcat was trying to find a firm grip with a rear paw, but his claws had hit a patch of old bark and rotted wood. Thumper, as if impatient with the delay, chose that moment to bark. The surprised stray turned to look. He slipped. Still, his reflexes were such that he managed to push out from the tree, twist while falling and throw Sleepy clear. The kitten landed headfirst on the bed of pine needles and old leaves. He was dazed.

The old stray landed on his feet. He was still strong and full of fight, ready to take on any kitten or any dog, but not two big dogs. And two big dogs were charging him at the precise moment of his landing. So the orange warrior turned and fled. He reached the nearest white pine first and scooted up its trunk just in the nick of time. If his tail had been its normal length, the leaping Duke's snapping jaws would have caught it.

Ten minutes later, a still-woozy Sleepy and the two dogs walked to the path and then followed it to the old stone wall and the house.

It was entirely possible that the orange cat who watched from high in the tree may have been Sleepy's father.

"Take it easy when you pet Sleepy," Cary warned her parents that night. "I think he has a sore neck."

"Don't look at me," said Pop. "I didn't wring it."

"No one is accusing you. I looked at you that way because I thought you might have a suggestion."

"Well, if I had a sore neck," Pop told his daughter, "I'd wrap a hot towel around it and go to bed."

"What about an aspirin?" asked Mom.

Cary saw more sense in her mother's suggestion, but—just to be on the safe side—she decided to phone Billy Hall and find out about the proper medicine.

"A sore neck? Do you mean a sore throat? Is it inflamed?" asked the cat expert.

"I mean a sore neck, or a stiff neck," Cary explained. "It seems to hurt him every time he moves his head."

Billy had cared for scores of ailing cats, but he wasn't familiar with stiff necks. He consulted his mother, and she confessed to the same lack of experience. So Billy returned to the phone and reported, "We think half an aspirin twice a day will do the trick."

The kitten was into his fifth month now and down to three meals a day. Half an aspirin was added to his first and last meals, and at the end of three days his neck was as normal as it had ever been. The people took the credit, but Sleepy had found his own cure: dozing in the sun for hours each day.

The heat of the sun provided the cure as the patient dozed atop the old stone wall. He just waited and dozed and listened, seemingly uninterested in hunting or exploring or journeying with the dogs. He had plenty of opportunity to join the dogs, for Duke and Thumper, separately and together, made frequent visits each day to the pine grove where they'd seen the orange cat. They didn't find the old stray, nor did they come across a fresh scent of him, and they lost all interest in their search after a few days.

It was a warm, sunny April day, so warm that Pop had been tempted to do a bit of spade work in the vegetable garden. The seeds wouldn't go into the ground for another month.

As he worked away, he saw Sleepy stroll across the lawn in the direction of the woods. "Don't climb any trees, and stay away from the birds," he shouted.

The kitten didn't pause or even look at Pop. He had squirrels on his mind and may have been hoping that he'd find them playing on the ground.

But what he found on the ground was in no way related to the rodent family. Before he was a hundred feet in the woods it came slithering down the path toward him. He'd never seen anything like it before: a long, thick thing with its entire body banded by blacks and golds. To Sleepy's eyes, of course, the bands were blacks and grays. A copperhead snake!

Nobody in his right mind plays with the poisonous copperhead. People don't and animals don't,

and kittens may be the only exceptions. A kitten considers a wiggling thing to be a plaything. A snake, or the first snake in a kitten's life, is a toy.

This one didn't hiss or coil or warn that he was danger. But the snake did come to a stop when its ears warned that something was approaching. A snake depends on hearing more than on seeing, its ears are tuned for ground vibrations, and its tongue is an even more sensitive finder.

The fat copperhead lifted its ugly head, and its tongue shot in and out of its jaws. Sleepy stopped, purred, then stepped forward for a closer look at the strange long thing. The snake hissed.

The kitten stepped backward and sat down, but he never took his eyes off the snake. The snake lowered its head, advanced a few inches, then raised its head again and shot out its tongue. Yes, that something was still in front, and now the object was retreating again.

The strange game between the kitten and the dangerous snake continued for almost half an hour. The snake advanced and stopped, the kitten retreated and stopped, and then the snake advanced again. The distance between them was never more than four feet, never less than three.

Finally the game came out of the woods and onto the open lawn. Sleepy made several more stops and retreats before Pop, still in the garden, noticed him and wondered what was going on. It was a full minute before he saw the copperhead.

Spade in hand, Pop jumped the garden fence and

hurried toward the snake. The copperhead couldn't see him, but the ground vibrations were strong and he was aware that a big something was coming his way. He coiled his long body. He was ready to strike!

Pop changed his mind. He wanted to destroy the snake, but he didn't want to come within the snake's range. Was there time to run to the house for his shotgun? He thought so. And would Sleepy be safe? Most likely. After all, Sleepy had been able to handle the snake thus far.

Pop ran to the house, and two minutes later he was back with his shotgun. From a safe distance of twenty feet he aimed at the still-coiled snake. An instant later Sleepy heard a mighty blast, and the copperhead was dead.

The sudden sound sent the kitten scurrying across the lawn and past the house. He raced into the garage and ducked behind a box in a corner, where he stayed until mealtime.

"Give him the best ground beef dinner that money can buy," Pop ordered. "Only the best is good enough for our snake charmer. Why, he may have saved our lives! I didn't know we had copperheads around here."

"Maybe Billy Hall is right," said Cary. "Maybe cats are smarter than dogs."

"On the other hand, maybe dogs are too sensible to fool around with poisonous snakes," Mom commented. She'd been a dog lover before Cary was born, and she knew it wouldn't do any harm to praise the dogs for a change. Besides, the kitten wouldn't need any more praise. She knew that for certain because she could read the new look on her husband's face: Pop had decided that Sleepy had won the right to become a permanent member of the family at Walden.

The sensible dogs may have wondered why Sleepy was served ground sirloin for dinner, while they had to settle for kibble and fish.

5

THE WATCHCAT

JUST as Cary and her mother had hoped, the gray-and-white snake charmer developed into a willing worker and earned his keep at Walden. It was an unhealthy spring for the mice in the basement, and for the rats in and around the garage and kennel.

There was no mystery as to who destroyed them. The well-fed Sleepy didn't make dinners out of his victims. Instead, he deposited them on the top step of the basement stairs, or on the stoop just outside the back door. The bodies were evidence of the kitten's successful labors, and not gifts to the dogs and those he loved.

The gray and white did not indulge in the sport of songbird hunting. He was interested in them and often played at stalking them, but—like more than half the cats in the world—made no attempt to add them to his diet. Bird meat is a last resort for many carnivorous animals, and is preferred only to starving. Animals haven't learned how to pluck feathers. Still, if Sleepy had been able to talk with words, he could have told Cary the position of every cardinal nest in the hemlock hedge, and the precise day the first eggs hatched.

He was a bit shy of his ninth month and on the verge of leaving kittenhood. He weighed twelve pounds, and was almost as big as he'd ever be. Looking at him, a stranger would have said that Sleepy was just like any other pet cat in the world. He looked like a cat, walked like a cat, and possessed the various talents of a cat.

But the stranger would have been wrong. While Sleepy was all cat and thus true to his family tree in every way, he also possessed some canine characteristics. In all his life he'd known just one cat, the old orange tom—and he hadn't been a friend. All of his animal friends had been dogs. He was a product of his environment, a law of nature endorsed by all scientists. Not half cat/half dog, but a cat who was sort of a copycat cat, or one who sometimes acted in the manner of a dog.

The people at Walden were aware of this, of course, although feline expert Billy Hall was the first to bring it to their attention. He had noticed that Sleepy would come from wherever he was when Cary called out the cat's name. That is, if Sleepy heard her.

It's a simple matter to train a dog to come when

called, but far more difficult to train a cat. And even then, there's no guarantee that a well-trained cat will come. He's an independent creature who bows to no man's will on a steady basis.

But Sleepy was so steady that Billy figured the gray and white didn't think of himself as a cat. Cary's cat was so used to being with dogs that he copied some of their habits. Coming when called was just one of them, and he didn't have to be rewarded with a meal or a snack or a word of praise. He was cooperative, not independent.

And he was as keen about swimming as the dogs. The stream below the cliff led to a small, deep pond in the woods, and Sleepy often went there on summer days with Thumper and his other canine friends. Unlike the Labrador, the cat isn't designed for swimming. He doesn't have the Lab's otterlike tail that comes in handy as a rudder. And he doesn't have the Lab's webbed feet that make for powerful strokes.

Nobody taught or encouraged Sleepy to swim, and it's hardly likely that he was envious of Thumper's talents in the water. On one particular day he simply followed the dogs into the water and started to swim. But it's likely that he had a little trouble if Folly was present, for Folly worried about anyone who wasn't a dog. She was forever trying to fetch swimming people ashore, and would have tried to carry the cat to safety. The yellow Lab didn't understand that healthy people and cats have the ability to swim.

Of all Sleepy's caninelike talents, the most important one went unobserved and unappreciated for the longest time. That was his ability to guard Walden against danger, and again it traced back to his association with the Labs. Whenever a stranger appeared at Walden, the dogs—indoors and out-doors—produced a chorus of barks. They considered a stranger to be anyone not a member of the family. Anything unfamiliar to them was also a stranger, such as a wild animal or the sound a stranger's car made as it came up the drive.

All during the growing season Sleepy was the sole guard of the vegetable garden. His tour of duty started around dawn. A three-foot wire fence en-closed the garden, but this barrier was more nuisance than defense against hungry enemies. Rab-bits dug under the fence, raccoons climbed over it, and deer jumped over it.

The deer were the last to attack. They waited until August when the corn was high enough to attract them. Three or four of the graceful creatures would arrive, plunder, and depart at some hour before dawn. They left their scent on the dew and Sleepy, who had never seen a deer, knew that some unknown enemy had come and gone.

On the second Sunday in August he sighted the unknown enemy for the first time. A young, greedy buck was still in the corn patch when dawn came and the cat arrived.

Sleepy remained outside the fence, but he was not frightened by the giant size of the enemy. He dropped to attack position: a crouch, with tail stiff and just the white tip of it barely waving. He was ready! He growled a challenge.

The young buck had noted the cat's approach. He wasn't concerned and paid no attention to the growl, although he did pause for a moment and look at Sleepy when the belligerent cat changed tactics and hissed.

One hundred feet away, the back door of the house opened and Cary, sleepy-eyed, stepped outdoors. It was destined to be another in a series of hot days, and Cary was up earlier than usual, intending to take a swim before breakfast. She wasn't looking toward the garden when she stepped outdoors and allowed the screen door to slam behind her.

But the buck heard the slam of the door and became frightened. He saw the girl as he soared over both the fence and Sleepy, and as he raced across the lawn he was completely unaware that the cat was running after him.

Cary saw the fleeing buck for no more than a few seconds. He seemed to fly over the grass and shoot over the stone wall before disappearing into the woods. The girl saw Sleepy for three seconds more. The cat was running at full speed in brave pursuit of the buck. Cary was so surprised that she didn't call out to her pet. She just stood with her mouth wide open as the cat jumped the wall and vanished into the woods.

"I can't believe my eyes!" she said, aloud and to herself. "Who ever heard of a cat chasing a deer?"

Two people who hadn't heard were her own parents. When, at breakfast, she told them about what she'd seen, both Mom and Pop looked at her skeptically. "I know it sounds silly," Cary repeated, "but I actually saw it happen! Honest!"

Mom smiled and suggested, "We were talking about how the deer are getting all the corn, remember? Just before you went to bed last night. Sure this wasn't a dream?"

"I pinched myself!" Cary insisted. "I wanted to make sure."

"We believe you," her father said. "We believe you because we must. Otherwise, your mother and I would go around hating ourselves for having failed to properly raise you. We've tried to teach you to be completely honest until you marry." He paused, tilted his head back and gazed at the ceiling before continuing, "Did I ever tell you about my pet canary? Her name was David."

"David is a boy's name," his wife reminded him.

"Yes, but I named her before I knew she was a girl canary. She didn't sing, but by the time I discovered that, she knew her name was David. Anyway, I was about ten, and a circus came to town. A mad elephant broke loose. His name was Goliath, and to make a long story short, the brute attacked our house. We were terrified! His charges shook the house to its foundations, and David's cage crashed to the floor. She escaped, flew out a broken window, and attacked Goliath. It was horrible, I tell you! She made mincemeat out of Goliath. And if you two think I'm kidding, a commemorative statue stands today in my hometown park. A huge stone elephant, and if you could lift one of his great stone ears, you would see David pecking away at a sensitive membrane."

Mom had not been listening. "I think we should have three cats," she said. "Each one could work an eight-hour shift, and all the vegetables would be safe."

Pop looked from Cary to his wife, and then back at Cary. "I knew there was a plot behind your story," he told his daughter. "Please keep your imagination in check. I still prefer having more dogs than cats around here."

He didn't quite believe her story about the deer chaser. After all, Sleepy was a pet cat, not a wildcat.

Pop was on the second week of his vacation and was hoping to live through another extremely hot day—the tenth in a row. It was so hot that he agreed to go swimming with his wife and daughter, a rare concession for a man who thought all bodies of water had been created solely for fishing.

They planned on swimming in the pond beyond the cliff, and since they wanted to swim and not be rescued, they left the house dogs at home. The Labs knew where their people were going, of course, and they were miffed at being left behind. They knew because the bathing suits were signals, just as the sound of clanking keys meant that somebody was about to take a trip in a car.

Sleepy remained with the house dogs. This was a practical measure, for no one knew he could swim.

And the new pups stayed at home, too. There were only four of them, and in three more days they would be six weeks old. Since there was no room for them in the kennel, they lived in a portable run and shed that had been set up adjacent to the garage. The run's fencing was five feet high, or high enough to keep the pups in and the big dogs out.

On Monday afternoon, just after the pups had downed their third meal of the day, Cary and her parents walked to the pond. All was peaceful at Walden. The shadow of the garage shaded the pups, so they slept in comfort. And it was cool in the house, so the big dogs and Sleepy were just as comfortable. Indeed, the cat knew supreme comfort. He dozed on Pop's favorite living room chair. It was a forbidden place for the cat and all the dogs, but Sleepy was unconcerned since Pop wasn't around.

The peace lasted for an hour. Then the kennel dogs started to bark: a sure sign that a stranger had arrived at Walden. Thumper trotted up the stairs to Cary's room. From one of her windows he had a clear view that extended from the garage to the kennel. The other house dogs and the cat waited below.

But they didn't wait long. They heard his deep growl grow into a single, angry bark. The dogs started for the stairs, then stopped as Thumper came bounding down, raced for the front door, and hurled his body against it. He wanted to get outdoors, and now the other dogs grasped his intent and sought other means of escape from the house. Thumper had sighted a dangerous stranger, and they intended to attack as an army.

Folly whimpered as she scratched away at one of the long windows. Old Duke headed for the kitchen and the closed back door. Chub raced up and down the stairs, growling and barking as if noise alone would produce a magical way out of the house. Moorborn dashed from window to window. She was the only methodical one, but her search was in vain. To keep the house as cool as possible, all the windows had been shut tight in the early morning hours.

Sleepy intended to get outside, too, and he knew just how to accomplish the deed. But first he had to wait for the frantic, milling dogs to grant him clear passage to the staircase. When Folly and Chub dashed down the hallway and Thumper was the only dog remaining in the room, the cat leaped from the chair, ran for the staircase, and hurried up the steps. Were the upstairs windows open?

Some of them were, but only because Cary had forgotten to close them. Just prior to leaving for their swim, her mother had told her to close those upstairs windows, for there was a strong possibility of afternoon showers. Cary had been upstairs anyway to find her bathing cap. She had to search for the cap, and forgot about the windows.

She'd been swimming for over a half hour when the appearance of sudden dark clouds overhead caused her to remember the windows. She'd started for home minutes before Sleepy jumped from the window to the terrace roof and worked his way to the ground. Now Cary was running down the path from the cliff, hoping to reach the house before the rain fell. Her mother was far to her rear, and her father was somewhere to the rear of her mother. He was strolling homeward in leisurely fashion, confident that it wouldn't rain.

And Sleepy was dashing for the puppy pen adjacent to the garage, where a stranger was menacing the pups!

The intruder was the biggest dog Sleepy had ever seen: Great Dane in size, but in other ways he didn't resemble any particular breed. There were scars across the muzzle of his huge wolfish head, and open sores on his legs. The mongrel's ribs showed through his short brown coat as if to advertise the fact that he hadn't been eating too well of late.

He'd arrived at Walden by both accident and design. The stray dog had been trotting through the woods, looking for trouble but headed for no particular destination. He'd caught the scent of a bitch in season and traced it to the kennel. There he'd been frustrated in his attempts to reach the bitch, and he'd become enraged at the strong kennel fencing. It had resisted his bites and he hadn't been able to scale it. And all the other Labs in the

kennel had barked insults at him from the safety of their runs.

None were aware that the big brown stranger was famous in the next county as a killer of calves and lambs and chickens, to say nothing of pet cats and dogs who got in his way. He'd been mean for a long time, and may have been the end result of a pup who had once been mistreated by people. In any event, he didn't trust man, and he didn't like anything or anyone who crossed his path.

The pups had yapped at him when he approached the house. If they'd kept quiet, he might not have noticed their presence. The angry mongrel had hurled himself against the fencing of the puppy run and found it just as unyielding as the wire at the kennel. Now, as Sleepy hurried toward him, he was attempting to dig under the fencing, and he was finding the digging difficult. The layer of tar was no problem, but the hard-packed stone underneath was unyielding.

His head was down and his rump was up when he first saw Sleepy, and for a few moments he stayed in that position. The mongrel's inaction was probably caused by surprise, for he'd never known a cat to openly seek an end to all nine lives at once.

The final moment proved too long, for Sleepy leaped and landed on the big dog's head. The cat went to work instantly, raking his claws along the dog's muzzle and cutting the skin above one eye. That brought a shriek of pain and a series of violent bucks from the dog, but he couldn't dislodge Sleepy.

The terrified pups were huddled in one corner of their run, and they were the only witnesses of the unusual war being waged ten feet away from them. The dog's huge jaws were his mightiest weapons, and he would win the war if he could bring them into action. But first he had to get the enemy off his head and within range of his jaws. He attempted to do just that by bashing his head against the fencing.

But Sleepy, as if reading the dog's intent, managed to twist free just before the headlong crash. His acrobatics sent him spinning to the pavement. As the confident dog turned and lunged at him, Sleepy scooted under the enemy's brown belly and raced for the nearest tree. He paused twenty feet up the trunk, first to catch his breath, and then to hiss and spit at the leaping mongrel below him.

For the moment, the war was at a standstill. The kennel dogs were quiet, and so were the house dogs. Up above, a black cloud blotted out the sun. Then, in the puppy pen, one of the foolish pups stood against the wire and uttered a series of soprano barks. His noise triggered a general outburst of more ominous barks from the kennel and the house.

Without so much as a glance at Sleepy, the brown dog gained his feet and walked toward the puppy pen. The four pups barked and crowded against the near side of the pen. Their tails were wagging, as if they had already forgotten that the approaching monster was not their friend.

Sleepy backed down the tree, then leaped the final five feet to the ground. From there he hurried after the dog. He snarled as he moved, trying to distract the giant and tempt him into another chase.

But the big dog seemed to pay no attention to the cat noises. He hurled himself against the puppy pen, but the wire didn't give. Then he attacked the wire with his claws and teeth until his gums bled and he could taste his own blood!

All of his actions may have been just a ruse to bring the cat closer. If so, it worked, for Sleepy was within ten feet of him when the dog suddenly turned and lunged.

Up above, a bolt of lightning ripped through the dark sky.

Cary ran across the lawn. She had heard the barking while still in the woods and knew that something was wrong. She was shouting at the top of her lungs, for she'd seen the big dog tearing at the puppy pen, but the lightning's crash echoed for miles around and drowned all other sounds.

"Run, Sleepy, run!" she shouted, but the cat didn't hear her. He sidestepped the lunging dog, twisted his body, crouched and leaped. The dog turned just in time for his nose to meet ten, sharp claws, all belonging to the gray and white's front paws.

The brown giant's tormentor dove under his chest. Again the dog turned and lunged, but Sleepy was safely away and running for the tree. The stranger barked his hatred, but he didn't pursue. It was as if he sensed that pursuit would be useless, and as if he felt the puppy pen couldn't withstand one more assault. Somebody would have to pay for the pain over his right eye, and for the blood staining the hair on his lower jaw. That somebody would be a pup, or all four of them!

He started for the puppy pen, then paused. He was aware of two new sounds. One of the barking dogs sounded closer than before. The dog was Thumper, still in the house but barking from his post at Cary's open window.

Cary ducked into the garage and picked up an iron garden rake. Now she was yelling at the dog and advancing on him. He turned his body, faced her, and growled.

Cary stopped right where she was, about twenty-five feet from the dog. She was holding the rake handle short, as if the rake was a baseball bat, and she hoped that she looked more formidable than she felt.

Moments before, she'd felt very confident, or at least brave. But now the bravery had gone down the drain, for she'd seen the blood on the dog's muzzle. She thought that the blood was Sleepy's. Now she was frightened.

The killer dog advanced a few steps, stopped and snarled. He could scent her fear. He knew she was frightened, and that she was another enemy. He advanced again and stopped again.

Cary's knuckles were white where her hands gripped the rake. She was aware that it would be foolish to run for the house, and she wasn't sure that she could make her feet obey anyway. She felt frozen in position, unable to move any part of her body, and she prayed that she could somehow bring the rake's iron teeth down on the dog's head at just the right time. But she wasn't sure that her arms and hands would obey her.

She didn't take her eyes off the brown dog, didn't dare turn to look at her own window when Thumper's barks of rage turned into a series of grunts. He had been trying to climb out the window, and had lifted the bottom half with his head before it had descended on his neck and trapped him. He wasn't in any danger of choking, but now the window was on his neck and he wasn't going anywhere.

Another bolt of lightning streaked through the sky, and the sudden light provided Cary with her first clear view of the head of the threatening dog. He looked bloodier and uglier than ever. Her fear increased, and the crash of thunder that rolled over Walden just then seemed strangely appropriate to the moment.

First the thunder brought light rain, and then it seemed to bring a powerful stream of water that smacked full force on the side of the ugly dog's wounded head.

The surprised dog jumped and turned away from Cary as the stream of water hit his sore nose. He whimpered and retreated a few steps, and then he yelped as the rake's handle banged into his quarters. Cary, taking advantage of the distraction, had thrown the rake with all her strength.

Now the cat was coming down the tree, the pups were yapping, and two people were shouting. The big dog tucked his tail between his legs and ran down the hill. Sleepy jumped to the ground and raced after him, but gave up the chase after a hundred feet or so.

The two shouting people were Cary and her mother. Mom had heard the Walden dogs barking, too, and she had hurried for the house and arrived in time to see Cary threatened by the brown dog. Mom had remembered what her daughter had forgotten: water is the best weapon to use against a mad or a fighting dog.

Mom had run around the side of the house, attached the garden hose to an outside tap, turned the faucet to full power, and then aimed the jet stream of water at the dog. She had done the right thing at just the right time.

As she ran to Cary, still holding the spouting hose, lightning crossed the sky again and thunder accompanied her steps. Cary ran to meet her, and as they hugged each other a heavy rain started to fall. They stood there in their bathing suits, as soaked as if they were still swimming in the pond, and for long moments they couldn't find any words.

Indeed, the first words came from Pop: "Are you two crazy?" He had finally arrived home, and was hurrying to them in an awkward trot. The cord around his old bathing trunks had broken, and he had to keep pulling up the trunks. "Are you two crazy?" he repeated as he joined his wife and daughter. "Don't you know it's raining? Are you trying to hold each other up? And what are you trying to water with the hose? The rain clouds?"

His girls were laughing and unable to reply. The laughter signified both their great relief and an appreciation of the picture they made. Both were drenched from the rain, and the water from the hose Mom still held spouted upward toward the sky before joining the rain and falling with it.

Pop was a practical man. He hurried to the outside tap and turned off the faucet. As he did so, he heard a whimper from above, and he looked up and saw the trapped Thumper.

So the head of the house was the one who dashed into the house and up the stairs to lift the window and release the yellow Lab. It was the least dangerous of a series of rescues on that day at Walden, but it was a rescue nonetheless.

6

MANHOOD

THE moon was full on a night in September. It was a warm night, and a restless Sleepy couldn't resist the temptation to visit the dark outdoors. Hours before dawn the cat left Cary's bedroom through the open window and traveled his long-established route to the ground.

Although two months shy of his first birthday, Sleepy was a full adult now, and as ready as he'd ever be to face the world. Manhood had been a long time coming, but it had arrived.

Something drew him to the path in the woods that led to the cliff. Once there, he crouched on a tree stump, stretched his neck as far as it would go, and tilted his head back and up. Then he started singing to the moon.

People have a name for the song: caterwauling. It is a strange sound, often compared to a dog's howl, although it has a wavering, weird quality that sets it apart. All sorts of myths are associated with caterwauling, and all are humbug, including the most popular myth of all: that a caterwauling pet cat means that somebody near and dear is dying. The truth—more often than not—is that the caterwauls of a male cat spell his need for romance.

Every few minutes Sleepy would interrupt his singing and listen. All he heard the first few times was a chorus of tree frogs and the distant, repeating hoots of an owl. It was a good half hour before he heard the answer he was unwittingly waiting for: the callings of a lady cat.

He'd heard the calls of lady cats before, but they'd never held any special meaning for him. On this night, however, the high-pitched series of wild cries did hold a meaning: the lady cat, whoever she was and wherever she was, was also in the mood for romance.

In fact, she was a good ten miles away. If Cary had been standing next to Sleepy she wouldn't have heard the distant callings. But a cat's sense of hearing is so acute that Sleepy heard, and heard distinctly. And so did every other cat who was within a ten-mile radius of the calling lady.

Sleepy wasn't aware of that, of course, as he jumped from the stump and started out on the longest trip of his life. Except for the visits with the Labs to the nearby pond, he'd never been away from Walden.

He proceeded to cross fields and hills and roads that were all unfamiliar to him. And every so often he would stop and listen for the lady cat's callings. Sometimes he would have to wait for minutes before he heard her calls, and they seemed so far away. But he continued to hear the calls and they were his beacons as he journeyed through the night toward the lady cat and dawn.

The calling lady was a beautiful red Persian with eyes of deep copper. She was a valuable animal: one year old and already a show champion. Her owner was very proud of her and planned to breed her properly at some time in the future.

Champion Red Rebel was not aware of those plans, and knowing them wouldn't have changed her present desire anyway. She was in both the mood and condition for romance, and she was quite willing to select her own mate. So she'd wandered away from her comfortable home and found a romantic setting in the ruins of an old barn on an abandoned farm. It was an ideal place for her purposes. All it lacked was a mate.

She climbed to the highest point of the ruins and voiced the first of many callings, and within the hour they produced the desired results: almost simultaneously, and from three different directions, three tomcats arrived. She saw them and they saw her, but none approached her. They kept their eyes on each other most of the time, for they were experienced toms and knew that the lady's choice of a mate was really up to them: all potential suitors would have to fight for the honor of winning her hand. The winner would claim her love.

Other male cats arrived from time to time, and by an hour before dawn more than twenty had assembled in the yard of the abandoned farm. Some were on low limbs of trees, some crouched on the remains of an old board fence, and others strutted on the ground. All hurled insults at each other, but the only fighting had been brief and amounted to no more than occasional sparring. No blood had been spilled, and Rebel was no longer calling. She was still where she had been atop the barn's ruins, carefully washing herself with her tongue and paying scant attention to her army of suitors. They were all colors and ages, although there wasn't a longhair among them. Most were pet cats, some were strays, and the oldest one present was a big orange with rounded ear tips and a stub of a tail.

It was an old story to the veteran stray. He was crouched on a low limb waiting for the battle royal to begin. His own plan of action was simple and based on previous successes: stay out of the fight until a weary winner emerged, then knock the stuffings out of the winner and claim the lady for

himself. He was conserving his strength for the right moment.

Unfortunately, Sleepy's approach to the barn brought him directly under the limb on which the veteran stray crouched. It's hardly likely that the old tom recognized him, but something—perhaps the gray and white's purring—infuriated him. He tensed, timed his leap perfectly, and dropped down on Sleepy with claws unsheathed.

The stray's claws missed the target, but his body slammed into Sleepy and knocked the gray and white to the ground. The old tom gained his feet first. He screamed and tore into the rolling, twisting Sleepy. A black tom came from nowhere and jumped the old orange, and then a gray tabby joined the action. Within seconds the yard exploded into a series of cat fights. All the toms had been waiting for somebody to start something, and now somebody had.

It was jungle warfare—not one battle, but a number of simultaneous battles, with some of the combatants dashing from one to another. Snarls, growls, hisses and screams mingled with cries of pain from the wounded.

Rebel sat with her tail wrapped around her, looking down upon the scene. It was bathed in the first gray light of dawn, and she could see it all, but she wasn't excited. As far as she was concerned, it was a perfectly natural happening and nothing to worry about. So long as one tom survived, she would be satisfied. She had no favorite.

At the end of ten minutes her suitors numbered

only four. All the others had either retired to the sidelines or had retreated from the farm. Sleepy was among those who had retreated. The surprise attack had stunned and confused him, and while he'd done his share of fighting, he'd received more punishment than he'd handed out. When he dragged himself away from the battlefield it was because he felt the need for rest was more important than the winning of the lady cat's favors.

The wounded soldier looked worse than his condition warranted, for not all of the bloody patches that stained his gray coat and white chest were caused by his own wounds. Indeed, the cuts he'd received were more like deep scratches, and his only really painful souvenir of the war was a half-inch cut that split the tip of his right ear. Time would heal the split, and hair would grow over it, so his handsomeness would not be marred.

Not far from the abandoned farm, Sleepy came to a brook. Fifteen minutes earlier, when he'd been traveling in the opposite direction, the cat had jumped the brook. Now he was content to lap the water and satisfy his thirst.

The drink made him feel better, but it didn't restore any strength to his body. Home was far away, and he didn't feel quite up to the journey. What he did feel like was some sleep.

His bed was the bare ground on the windless side of a sheltering rock. He curled his body into a tight ball, brought the tip of his tail over his nose, and succumbed to deep sleep.

The sleep lasted for hours. When the cat awakened it was late afternoon and time to begin the return journey to Walden. The right ear still throbbed, and now all of his muscles were stiff and sore. He loosened them a bit by washing himself with his tongue until his coat was presentable. The labor left a bitter taste of dried blood in his mouth, and this he washed away with a drink from the brook. Finally he was ready for the journey home.

He didn't jump the brook this time. Instead, he waded through the shallow water, paused just long enough on the far bank to determine his bearings, then hurried off in a westward direction through woods that would lead to miles of open farming country.

Sleepy was ten miles from Walden. Some instinct told him that he was traversing the same course, although in the opposite direction, that he had followed in the dark hours before dawn. Scientists call this a homing instinct. Many animals possess it, and cat experts agree that it is strongest of all in the cat. There are scores of stories to substantiate their belief: stories of cats who have traveled hundreds and even thousands of miles to reach their homes and masters. The cats can't read maps and seem to find their way by magic, as if each was equipped with built-in radar. Of course, the belief of the cat experts does not alter the fact that some cats get lost when they are barely out of sight of their homes. Homing instincts are not infallible.

If Sleepy possessed the homing instinct it had been jarred by the fighting at dawn. Walden lay southward, and he was traveling westward, and his every step widened the distance between himself and home.

———————⌣———————

Cary didn't become concerned about Sleepy's whereabouts until she arrived home from school. She had not seen him in the morning, but there was nothing unusual about that. He was often outdoors exploring in the woods by the time she awakened, so she didn't always see him before she left for school.

But the cat and Thumper were usually waiting for her at the foot of the drive when she stepped off the school bus at four-thirty in the afternoon. They would escort her up the long driveway to the house, with Sleepy meowing most of the way. He had reached the one-meal-a-day stage, and Cary always prepared and served it to him at about five.

"Where's Sleepy?" the girl asked Thumper when she found only half the welcoming committee on hand that afternoon. The dog's reply was a furious wagging of his tail, and that told her nothing.

She found her mother in the vegetable garden. Mom also didn't know where Sleepy was. "Come to think of it, I haven't seen him all day," she told her daughter. "But he'll show up soon. He knows when it's mealtime."

Cary went into the house and prepared his dinner, but the missing cat remained missing. Every ten minutes or so Cary went outdoors and called his name several times, but still he didn't appear. And an hour before dusk, she and three of the house dogs—Duke, Thumper, and Folly—started on a search of the woods. They didn't find Sleepy.

"We'll search again in the morning," Cary announced at the dinner table. "He must be somewhere. Maybe he's trapped."

"Did you look around the old walled spring?" asked Pop. "I saw him stalking a chipmunk there last Sunday."

"Gosh-I-forgot-the-spring-gosh-he-may-be-drowning-may-I-be-excused," said Cary, running the words together and not waiting for permission to leave the table. She ran down the hallway, grabbed a flashlight from the table, and dashed out the back door of the house. The spring was three hundred feet from the house and she ran all the way. It was a spring-fed well, really, and it had supplied drinking water for Walden long before the artesian well had been drilled. Any cat—or any dog or person, for that matter—who fell into the well would not escape without help.

Cary had to thrash through underbrush as she approached the well, and she could hear splashes as she came close. Were the splashes made by Sleepy or by the frogs who lived in the well? She found out as soon as she played the beam of the flashlight down into the well. Frogs!

"At least he didn't drown in the old well," Cary reported to her parents. "But don't you think it would be a good idea to put a cover over it? I think I'll make one."

"I wish you would," said Mom. "Your father has been intending to do it for ten years."

"The frogs do enjoy living there," mumbled Pop, "and frogs get such little pleasure out of life. The amphibians have as much right to enjoy life as dogs and cats." Then he turned to Cary and advised: "Now don't worry. Any cat who can beat up a dog and charm a copperhead can certainly take care of himself. He'll show up in a day or so. He's a big boy now and I have a hunch he's off on a peculiar adventure."

"Maybe," Cary replied. "Well, I think I'll phone Billy. He should have some advice."

As soon as her daughter left the room, Mom asked, "What did you mean by those two words?"

"What two words?"

"Peculiar adventure, quote unquote."

"Oh, those," said Pop. "Added together, they mean romance. Sleepy is about ten months old, right? I'm surprised he hasn't found a girl friend before this."

"The nearest female cats belong to the Halls, and Mrs. Hall keeps them under lock and key, so to speak."

"You've forgotten that a man will go a great distance to court his true love," Pop reminded her. "Why, you must have lived at least a half mile from me."

His thinking was correct, but he couldn't prove

it, of course. It was one of several thoughts that Billy Hall had, too, but he didn't mention them to Cary. If Sleepy had decided to do some exploring away from Walden, he might have been hit by a car, or shot by somebody who takes pleasure in shooting cats, or stolen. With so many free kittens and cats available, stealing one would seem unnecessary, but the fact remains that close to one million cats are stolen in this country every year by people who sell them to medical research laboratories.

But Billy Hall didn't want to worry Cary with any of the dire possibilities. Instead, he told her not to worry and assured her that Sleepy was close by somewhere, and to notify everybody she could think of, including the police, the vet, and the humane society.

Cary repeated his advice to her parents, and Mom promised to phone the authorities the next morning. And Pop came through with some sound advice. "If Sleepy is still missing, ask your teachers to make an announcement in every class."

The gray and white was still missing when morning arrived. Cary was up at dawn to search the woods with all five house dogs, but again the mission was in vain. And she missed the school bus.

After a hurried breakfast, Mom drove her to school. But it proved to be a lost academic day for Cary since her mind was on the missing cat and not on her studies. All her thoughts weren't in vain, however, for Sleepy was on his way home.

There was nothing wrong with his intentions,

but there was plenty wrong with his sense of direction. He was wandering in circles. And he was hungry. He'd enjoyed his last square meal at Walden almost forty hours before, and had made no attempt to find food on his own. It had never been necessary for him to forage, and only desperation would cause him to do so now. Like any cat, he could go for days without food, so long as he could find water.

So Sleepy was hungry but not desperately so, and he was taking care of himself by conserving his strength. He rested frequently, and spent those times studying the landscape and deciding which way to turn next. Home was somewhere, perhaps around the next curve or over the next hill, although all the scenery looked unfamiliar to him. But by the second night, home was twenty-five miles away.

Long after darkness had settled the cat heard dogs barking in the distance. He hurried down a dirt road in the direction of those barks, quite sure that he had finally found Walden.

But the dogs he was so anxious to join weren't his friends the Labradors. There were three of them filling the night with their din, and all three were oversized Doberman Pinschers.

They were standing outside the back door of a farmhouse. Their master was inside the house, and as far as he was concerned, they could bark all night. He fed them every other night, and this wasn't the night.

"Listen to the stubborn fools," the farmer said to

his mother. He was sitting at the kitchen table reading the weekly paper, while his mother washed the supper dishes. "They know they don't get fed tonight. Listen to the fools."

"I can hear them without listening," said his mother. She was almost ninety. A tiny, frail woman, she stood looking out the window as she worked, watching the three dogs in the light that spread out from the kitchen windows. "I just don't understand you," she said to her sixty-year-old son. "Dogs should be fed every day. If your father was still alive, he'd spank you. He loved dogs."

"I'm smarter than he was," her son replied without taking his eyes off the paper. His narrow nose and close-set eyes seemed out of place on his round face, and his mouth wore a crooked smile. "They stole from him but they'll never steal from me, and don't ever forget that!" He was not referring to his dogs, but to almost every other living thing: the fox and weasels that might raid his hen houses, the raccoons and deer and rabbits that might sample his crops, the rats that might steal from his corn cribs, the crows that might dig up his seeds, and even strangers who might steal his cows.

He owned the three Dobes so that they could guard his treasures. He kept them hungry and mean so that they would be on the alert against real and imaginary thieves. For miles around, everybody knew about the dogs and stayed clear of the farm.

"You hear what I said?" he asked.

"I heard," was his mother's answer. Usually she

scolded him when he berated his late father, but now she wanted him to stop talking and reading and go to bed. He always retired at nine o'clock sharp, and the kitchen clock read ten minutes shy of that hour.

Something was happening outdoors that she didn't want him to see, so she said, "Fix the clock before you go to bed, it's ten minutes slow."

The trick worked. Her son looked at the clock, yawned, pushed his chair back, and crossed the room to the wall clock. He pushed the minute hand ahead to nine, then walked out of the room. "The paper says we've got chicken thieves around again. Floyd Haskell lost three hundred hens on Monday night," were his parting words. He didn't say goodnight.

"Goodnight," his mother said. As she listened to his steps going up the stairs to his bedroom, she was watching the scene outdoors. The three hungry Dobes were pacing back and forth in front of the back door and her window, barking at each other and at the door and at the window. And twenty feet to their rear a gray-and-white cat was sitting. The dogs hadn't noticed the cat.

The old woman rapped on the window. She was telling Sleepy to run while there was still time, but the barks drowned out the raps on the glass. And then, as she watched, the dogs stopped barking and all three came to a halt. They had heard something!

For just a moment the big red dogs were statues, as if they couldn't believe that a cat was so close. Then one turned his head and saw Sleepy. He growled, and the growl was a command to his companions. All three wheeled about and lunged for Sleepy! In a military sense, the canine charge was an awkward one, for the dogs bumped into one another.

The growl and the charge told Sleepy all that he needed to know: the dogs were not friendly. The cat turned and leaped in one continuous motion. His claws dug into the trunk of an old apple tree and he scampered up the trunk in the nick of time. The reaching jaws missed his tail by less than an inch.

The gray and white crouched on a limb and watched the dogs below him. They stood there and looked up, wagging their tails and whimpering, but the wags and the whimpers meant anxiety and not friendship. The big red dogs were hungry enough to eat cat, and Sleepy seemed to understand that. So he stayed where he was—twenty feet above their heads, safe and sound on the limb of an apple tree.

The back door opened and the old woman came out of the house. She was carrying three bowls of food, one for each dog. She did the same every other night after her son went to bed, but she never told him.

When she appeared the dogs forgot about Sleepy and trotted to her. "Mind your manners and don't be in such a hurry to eat," she said to the dogs. "Tonight you're going to eat in the barn." She didn't put the bowls down until they were inside the barn. While they were gulping their meals, she closed the door and latched it.

She walked back to the house. "I'll be back in a minute," she said as she passed the apple tree. Her words were not meant for the tree. They were meant for the cat in the tree.

The old woman disappeared into the house. A long minute later she returned to the apple tree with a dish full of chopped beef and a bowl of milk. She placed the dish and the bowl on the ground, backed off a few steps to look up at Sleepy, then turned and walked back into the house.

Sleepy stayed right where he was for another half hour. By then the dogs were barking again, but their sounds were muffled and the dogs themselves didn't appear.

The gray and white finally came down from the tree and circled the dish and the bowl. He crouched before the dish, looked in every direction, extended his neck, and sampled the meat. After that first taste, the cat tore into the meat, bolting it down in hurried fashion, as if racing against time. Sleepy had never eaten so much so quickly, but he'd never been so hungry. The milk was fresh, but it was too cold for his taste buds. A half dozen laps satisfied him.

He didn't know that the old woman was watching him from the kitchen window. When she rapped on the window she was telling him to finish the milk. But the unexpected sound frightened him, and he ran off across the yard and into the darkness.

The cat slowed to a walk when he hit the dirt road. His belly was full, he felt fine, and he didn't intend to stop until he reached home, wherever that was. But it was somewhere, and he'd keep going until he found it.

The road crested a hill, and Sleepy—walking right down the middle of it—could see miles ahead into a valley. Lights seemed to race back and forth in the valley, and he could hear the noises they made. The lights and the sounds were familiar to Sleepy. Headlights and motors, of course. He had no words for them, but he'd seen and heard them many times on nights when he'd look out Cary's window to the highway in the valley.

The cat broke into a trot and then a pace. In deed he was hurrying homeward, but not in fact.

7

THE TWO-DOLLAR STRAY

"HAVE you advertised?" Billy asked in school the next morning. When Cary answered negatively, he added, "Well, it doesn't cost much and it might bring results. People have been known to hold cats and dogs in the hope of getting a reward."

Cary thought it was a good idea, and she made a mental note to suggest it at the dinner table that night. But the suggestion wasn't necessary, for as soon as she reached home that afternoon, her mother announced, "Still no word about Sleepy, so I placed an ad in both the daily and weekly papers."

"Did you offer a reward?"

"Yes, and I added the words 'young owner heartbroken.' I also telephoned the radio station. There's a program about missing pets every morning at ten. There's no charge for the first week."

"I wonder if there's anything else we can do to find him?"

Mom shook her head. "I didn't tell you, but I spent an hour yesterday and two hours today driving up and down back roads and asking everybody I saw. I think the whole county is on the alert by this time. Oh, can you find the time to feed the pups and the house dogs?"

Later, after Cary had fed the pups and played with them, she told them not to worry about Sleepy. They weren't worried about anything or anybody, and what she said was really designed to bolster her own confidence: "We still haven't found Sleepy, but don't worry. Everybody is looking for him, and we're advertising, and sooner or later we'll find him, or somebody will. And whoever finds him will notify us."

Part of her wish was already fulfilled, for Sleepy had been found! But the finder would never read the newspapers or hear the radio program carrying the news about the missing cat.

The chain of events leading to the finding of Sleepy had started at an early hour in the morning. He had reached the highway before midnight, decided to cross it, and then voted against the idea. The big monsters with the blazing eyes and roaring voices came racing along much too frequently, and it seemed silly to challenge them. So the cat walked along on his own side of the highway, and—for a change—he was walking in the right direction. A thirty-mile walk down the highway would bring him within two miles of Walden.

It was the first cold night of September. Clouds hid the moon and the stars. The cat's progress was slow, for he paused frequently to look around and make sure that the blazing lights weren't searching for him. And then it started to rain.

He was wet and weary when a long, low building appeared up ahead. The building was bursting with light. It was an all-night diner, and a panel truck was parked in front of it. The driver had been so anxious for a cup of coffee that he'd left the cab door open.

The open door was like an open invitation. Sleepy jumped onto the driver's seat. It was dry in the cab, but the seat was cold. He tried the passenger seat, but that was cold, too. He jumped to the floor and found it warm. And it was still warmer under the passenger seat. That's where he curled up and fell asleep.

He awakened but made no attempt to stir and announce his presence when the driver returned to the truck and started the motor. The well-fed, weary cat fell into a deep sleep as the truck roared down the highway. He was warm and comfortable on the floor, and the vibrations disturbed him no more than the truck driver's voice, or not at all. In an effort to keep awake, the man sang cowboy songs at the top of his lungs.

Ninety minutes later the sleeping cat and the singing man sped past a point that was precisely two miles from Walden. But the truck didn't turn down the road that led to the cat's home. It went straight on for another five miles, then swung westward.

Sleepy was still in slumberland when the truck crossed a river. He didn't awaken until dawn, when the truck stopped at a warehouse on the fringes of a city. Earlier, he had been two miles from home. Now he was more than eighty.

The driver climbed out of the cab, went to the back of his truck, opened the doors, and started to unload the cargo. Sleepy crawled free of his bed, hopped onto the passenger seat, stretched and yawned. Then he looked out the window. The scenery was not familiar.

Both of the cab doors were closed, but the driver's window was open. Sleepy jumped through it, hit the ground, and started to walk away. A moment later his feet were off the ground and he found himself in the arms of a strange man.

"Is this your cat?" asked the man. He was a policeman.

"No," said the truck driver.

"Then what was he doing in your truck?" asked the officer.

The driver shrugged and replied, "I never saw him before in my life. Believe me, I don't own a cat!"

"Now don't get excited. If he's your cat, why fine.

If not, then he's a stray and he goes to the city pound, and you know what that means. So for the last time, is this your cat?"

"No. And if a camel jumps out of my truck, you can have him, too. I don't own a camel. Now, do you mind if I get on with earning a living?"

"I hate to do this," said the man of the law, "but if I bring home one more cat, my wife will leave me."

So Sleepy traveled to the city pound in a radio patrol car. There, after a great deal of horn blowing, he was delivered into the hands of the biggest, fattest man he'd ever seen. The man was the dog warden, but he was also responsible for any kind of a lost or stray animal.

"I wish you cops would forget about stray cats and concentrate on bank robbers," said the fat man. "I've got fifty of 'em here already."

He wasn't exaggerating. The wire pen that became Sleepy's new home contained about five dozen roommates, and all were constant complainers. They hated their prison, and the only time they quieted down was once a day, when they were fed.

None of them paid any attention to the gray-and-white newcomer. Each of the cats was concerned only with himself and with what the future held in store. All wanted to be free, and all would have shrieked night and day if they'd known about the future, for it wasn't very promising. A few would be claimed by their owners, a few would be saved by new owners, but most would be destroyed.

Each of the cats was considered a stray, and each was supposed to be held for ten days before the sentence of death was bestowed. But it was a risky ten days, for the warden didn't keep individual records and some cats looked just like others. So when he had too many, he simply removed a few from the pen and destroyed them. "Too many" was an arbitrary figure in his mind, and it changed from time to time. On days when he couldn't stand the feline clamor any longer, he would remove a dozen or so cats, place them in his homemade gas chamber, and turn on the gas.

So from the very first hour of his imprisonment in the city pound, Sleepy's life was in danger. He was one of the few prisoners who had a real owner, but his owner didn't know where he was.

Despite departures every few days, the cat population at the city pound remained about the same. It was a rare day when at least one newcomer wasn't tossed into the pen.

It didn't take Sleepy long to learn that it wasn't safe to be greedy. Sometimes the first cats who rushed to the feeding pans were grabbed by the warden and placed in a box. Those cats were never seen again.

At feeding time Sleepy crouched in a far corner of the pen, as far away from the fat man as possible. The cat didn't approach the feeding pans until he was sure the man had left both the pen and the room. By that time there wasn't much food left, but usually the other cats had overlooked a few scraps, and Sleepy was grateful for anything he could find.

And then, early on the morning of Sleepy's sixth day at the city pound, a man stopped outside the pen. He spent a long time studying the cats. The cats had never seen him before, but the warden had. Indeed, almost everybody in the city had seen the man and knew him as Hermit Jake.

He was tall, thin, and bearded, and he wore his hair long. His clothes were tattered, and his shoes were tightly wrapped rags. Some little children would run and hide when they saw him coming, which wasn't often. He visited the city three or four times a year, walking the ten miles from his one-room shack in the hills near the state forest. He bought provisions on those trips—such necessities as flour, salt, thread, needles, and pans—and always paid for them in cash. How Hermit Jake obtained the money and what his real name was had been a local mystery for over fifteen years.

Jake took his time looking over all the cats in the pen before calling out, "I found the right one!"

The warden came into the room and asked, "You have enough money? Two dollars?"

Jake didn't say anything. Instead, he reached into his pocket, withdrew a handful of nickels, dimes, and pennies, and gave the coins to the warden. The fat man counted the change and said, "You're a dime short."

The hermit handed over another ten pennies, then pointed at Sleepy and said, "The gray and white."

"You sure know your cats, Jake," said the warden. "I've sort of been holding on to that one for an aunt of mine. He's been here for over a month." He was lying, of course, but he didn't want to lose a sale. The money would be all his. "Go right in and help yourself."

Hermit Jake entered the wire enclosure with the warden's net in his hand. The cats scattered, and Sleepy huddled in his favorite corner. He didn't move as the net descended over his head and body, nor did he attempt to escape when the man grabbed him by the scruff of the neck. It was a new, puzzling experience for Sleepy, and he didn't know how to react.

Jake used a cardboard carton that had once contained bars of soap as a carrying case for the cat. The man closed the flaps and tied them down with string. Sleepy had plenty of air to breathe, but he didn't see daylight again until that afternoon when the man opened the carton on the floor of his shack.

While his new owner sat on a box and watched, Sleepy stuck his head out of the carton and looked around the room. The room was small, with a door at one end, a stone fireplace at the other end, and a small window on each of the two facing walls. Opposite corners of the room were piled high with a jumble of cartons, crates, bundles of old newspapers, wads of rags, coils of wire, and odd pieces of tin. These were all things that Jake figured he might need some day. The pieces of tin, for example, would come in handy for patching the roof.

One of the windows was almost hidden by a stack of three old mattresses tied together and standing against the wall. Along the opposite wall was Jake's bed: another old mattress resting on a rusty, metal bed frame, and the frame resting on four wooden boxes. A crude table, a stool, three boxes, and a small iron stove were the only other furnishings in the room. The stove wasn't used for cooking, but for storing any extra food. It was the only way Jake could protect the food from the mice.

Of the many scents that greeted Sleepy's nose, the strongest was that of field mice. The room was full of them and always had been, and Jake had never figured out a way of getting rid of his unwelcome guests. He could have burned his shack, of course, but then he would have had to build another, and he wasn't an ambitious man. And he could have cleaned up the place and thus rid the room of its hiding places, but neatness was not one of his virtues. The easy solution was always the best one for Jake, and finally he'd decided that the best solution for getting rid of the mice was to acquire a cat. He had never liked cats, but he preferred them to mice.

Now, as Sleepy jumped from the carton and started a cautious, step-by-step investigation of the room, Hermit Jake talked to him: "I'll tell you why I bought you, Mister Cat. My castle is overrun with mice, and I expect you to catch and kill every one of them. You may get tired of eating them, but that will be your tough luck, for I don't intend to feed you anything else. Back of the stove you'll find a shallow box filled with sand. Use that when nature calls, because I'm not going to let you go outdoors until all the mice are gone." He paused. It was obvious to him that the cat wasn't listening.

"Don't be a fool," he continued. "I'm not in the habit of repeating myself. Do you hear me, Mister Cat? Are you listening, damn you!" The last five words were shouted. Sleepy stopped and looked at him. "That's better," said Jake. "It may flatter you to know just why I selected you from that gang of idiot cats at the city pound. You're big and strong, of course, but what I liked most about you was the pattern on your forehead. The dark lines run together to form the letter *M*. That means you go back through history to the earliest pet cats. The Egyptian word for cat is maou, you see, and the people knew that *M* also meant mighty mouser."

Sleepy didn't know what Jake was talking about, but Billy Hall would have agreed with the man. Hermit Jake, for all his strange ways, read books when he could find them, and the last one he'd found in the county dump had been about the history of cats.

The hermit did not believe in work of any kind. Out of necessity he compromised his philosophy by only working at the finding of food and drink. But he considered such labors to be sports. No matter the legal trapping season, he was an expert at snaring small game animals and birds on a year-round basis, and he knew just which wild plants made the best vegetables, and which tubers could be stored away for winter cooking. And one of his annual pleasures was the harvesting of such wild fruits as elderberries, huckleberries, and fox grapes. All made excellent wines, and Jake made enough wine each fall to satisfy the wants of several average wine lovers.

On some nights he would sing himself to sleep. It was always the same song and consisted of five words: "I'm wining myself to sleep." He would repeat the phrase over and over—with time out only for more sips of wine—until he fell asleep. It was his way of forgetting the past, and perhaps of forgetting the mice.

Thus Sleepy's new home amounted to no more than another prison, and he was worse off than he had been before. His new warden didn't feed him, and the warden was drunk every night.

The cat was a veteran hunter of mice, rats, and moles. He had gained his experience at Walden, but there he'd been well fed and had never felt obliged to dine on rodent.

He was well aware that his new prison was mice-abundant. He could scent them at any hour of the day or night, and he could see them when he was alone in the shack and stayed quiet. They were in the heaps of corner rubbish, on the junk-filled shelves over the fireplace, under the stove and in the mattresses. For them, the shack was a fun house and not a prison, for they were at liberty to come and go as they pleased through the holes in the floor and walls that Jake had neglected to stuff with rags.

The mice knew that the cat was there, but their natural fear of him soon faded away. As the days passed they grew bolder, and sometimes they played their games within a few feet of him. Sleepy would watch them, but he made no attempt to slaughter them, and his inactivity infuriated Jake. Every night the man would sit on his bed, sip from a jug of wine, and deliver a lecture to the cat: "You're the stupidest cat I've ever known! Why, you're more stupid than people who work for a living. How many times do I have to tell you that I'm not going to feed you? If you don't eat mice, then you'll starve to death. And when that happens, your friends the mice will eat you!" Jake usually ended up swearing at Sleepy, drinking more wine, and falling asleep.

So long as Sleepy had water, he was in no real danger of starving—and Jake always kept a pail of water near the fireplace for cooking purposes. The cat would drink when the man wasn't present, or when the man was asleep. So while the gray and white's hunger increased, so did his streak of stubbornness. He was interested in only one thing: escape. But the solid door was his only means of escape, and Jake was always careful when opening and closing it.

The pattern of the days and nights did not change until late afternoon on the tenth day. It was cold and Jake had a fire going. Sleepy was curled on the floor near the fireplace. The cat was dozing, and to the man he seemed the picture of contentment.

Jake was sitting on his bed with a jug of wine on his lap. He'd started drinking earlier than usual, and the wine didn't help his mood. The more he watched the contented cat, the more his anger grew. He started cursing himself aloud for having wasted his money on such a stupid cat, and then he started cursing the cat. Sleepy looked at him through half-opened eyes, but he didn't move or make a sound.

Two mice scurried across the room and passed within a yard of the cat before ducking under the stove. Sleepy's utter disinterest in the little rodents triggered the hermit's fury. He threw the jug of wine at the cat!

His aim was wild. The jug crashed into the fireplace above Sleepy's head. The cat scrambled to his feet, raced across the room, and jumped to the top of a corner rubbish heap. He was unharmed, although his coat had been drenched by elderberry wine.

Jake staggered across the room, picked up a box, and tossed it at the cat. Again his aim was wild, but he did hit the rubbish heap, and as it collapsed the cat leaped to the floor and raced for the opposite

corner of the room. The drunken man picked up the stool and hurled it at the gray and white.

The stool crashed through the window over Jake's bed. Cold air rushed into the room as Jake rolled up his sleeves and staggered toward the cat. "I'm going to wring your stupid neck!" he shouted as he bumped into the table. It looked to Sleepy as if the table had bumped into the man, for the man crashed to the floor.

The cat didn't wait for any more threats. He jumped on top of the bed and from there leaped through the broken window. And he didn't pause when his feet hit the ground outdoors. Instead, he raced for the nearest patch of woods. Once there, he didn't slow his speed. He was afraid that Jake would pursue him. But Jake was sitting on the floor of the shack and singing, "I'm wining myself to sleep." He held a new jug of wine on his lap.

Two miles from the shack Sleepy found a road straight in front of him and a house one hundred yards to his left. It was dusk by then, and as he approached the house an outside light came on. A door opened, and a woman and a dog appeared. She placed a dish of food on the porch, then turned and went back into the house. The dog put his head down and started to eat.

Sleepy walked across the yard and up the steps to the porch. He stopped about ten feet from the dog and meowed. The cat was hungry and anxious to share the food.

The old Cocker Spaniel was overweight and his vision was failing, but there was nothing wrong with his hearing. He put his head up and moved back from his meal. He growled, and Sleepy hissed right back at him.

The old dog made an awkward leap for the cat, but Sleepy had twisted and jumped down the steps to safety. His easy escape angered the Spaniel. In his younger days he had made a specialty of chasing cats. Now the old dog growled again and charged down the steps.

It was the beginning of a long chase, and from the start the proud dog didn't have a chance of overtaking the cat. Sleepy was younger and stronger, and his vision was better in the darkness. As they headed down the road he stayed well ahead of the pursuing dog. Indeed, several times he stopped and waited for the dog to come closer.

Finally, when the old, fat dog sat down to rest, Sleepy jumped a wall and changed direction. He headed back to the house and the dog's dinner on the back porch!

The gray and white was nowhere in sight an hour later when the weary dog returned to his home. His dinner dish was there, but there was no dinner in it.

When the back door opened and his mistress called him inside for the night, the old cocker had no way of telling her that he was still hungry. He didn't know who had stolen his food, or that the gray-and-white robber was sound asleep under the porch.

Thanks to the square meal and a good night's sleep, Sleepy felt better than he had in a long time. He awakened at dawn and wasted no time crawling out from his shelter and becoming the only traffic on the road he'd traveled the night before. It was as if all of his troubles in recent weeks had somehow adjusted his personal compass. For a change, his nose was pointed toward home. All he had to do to reach Walden was to stay on course for seventy miles, and also cross a river.

When the road seemed to bend the wrong way, he left it and journeyed cross-country. He walked most of the time, refreshed himself at several brooks, napped briefly in the afternoon, and covered about ten miles by dusk. The mileage brought him back to the western bank of the river he had crossed in the truck, and there he found a grove of old hemlocks. The carpet of needles was thick underfoot. Sleepy dug a nest in the carpet, curled up, and fell asleep.

It was not an uninterrupted sleep. Several times during the night he awoke and listened to the sound of dogs. What he heard were the bays of a running pack of hounds. But the sounds were always in the distance. Sleepy felt safe.

The sun was high in the sky when he stirred from his nest and went down the bank to the river. He had work to do, but first he wanted a drink. Then, after he satisfied his thirst, he wandered along the shore until he found a boulder suitable for his purposes. The one he selected was three feet off shore and had a flat top. He jumped across the water and landed on it. Sitting there, he had a clear view in every direction. The hounds he'd heard during the night were baying again, and they seemed to be coming closer.

He sat there for a few minutes, listening to the dogs and enjoying the warmth of the sun. Then he settled down to the work that had to be done: washing himself. As he worked with his tongue on one side of his coat, an overturned rowboat drifted slowly downstream. The boat's bottom was about two inches above water level, and smack in the middle of it sat a very wet cat. She was the reason why the hounds were coming closer.

The five hounds belonged to a farmer and his son who lived upriver. The dogs had been chasing rabbits and treeing raccoons all during the night, and the fact that their hunting had been in vain had not lessened their enjoyment. They were sort of getting in training for the legal hunting season, which was still weeks away.

At about the time Sleepy had awakened, the hounds had had enough fun and started for home. In the middle of an open field they'd come upon a stray cat. She was dining on a rabbit she'd stalked and killed, and the hounds may have regarded this as an insult to their own skills. They charged her and she fled.

The chase went across the field and down the bank to the river. Two hounds flanked her and made sure that she didn't head for the woods. So when she reached the river, it was a matter of fighting or swimming.

The lady cat was not a fool. She weighed a scant six pounds, and in all her four years her experiences with dogs had been limited to one dog at a time. The five hounds looked like five unbeatable giants to her, so she leaped into the water and started paddling for the far shore. The hounds waded a few feet from the bank, but the water was cold and they preferred dry land. They didn't follow her.

She was a blue-eyed shorthair, pure white except for a solid black left ear and three black ticks on her nose. Her name was Izzy, which was short for Isabelle, and it had been given to her by a little girl. That had been a long time ago, when she'd been just a kitten, and she'd forgotten about the name and the girl, and even where she'd lived. Now her only concerns were today and tomorrow, and what food and possible comforts they might bring.

Part way across the river, Izzy found the drifting rowboat. She climbed aboard, happy to leave the cold water, and happier when she saw that the hounds had not followed her. They were watching from the bank as they walked downstream, perhaps in the hope that the currents would push ashore Izzy's upside-down yacht.

Sleepy had almost finished his bath when the hounds came into view. He crouched, hoping to make himself as small as possible.

The hounds were still fifty feet away when the smallest one stopped, put his nose to the ground, and picked up Sleepy's scent. The dog barked, announcing his discovery, and charged ahead with his nose still to the ground. His four companions barked excitedly and raced after him. As the crouching cat watched, the whole pack sped right past him.

Then all five bumped into one another. They'd lost Sleepy's scent, and all five had tried to stop and turn at the same time. As they walked back toward Sleepy, he tried to crouch lower into the boulder, but he couldn't dent it.

The lead hound stopped on the shore where Sleepy had leaped to the boulder. The dog looked up and saw the crouching cat. He woofed. It wasn't much of a sound, sort of a clearing of the throat, but it brought his companions to the alert—and they saw Sleepy!

An instant later all five were jumping for the boulder and Sleepy! For the second time that morning, the hounds forced a cat to make an instant decision: fight or swim. The gray and white voted for swimming. He twisted, leaped, and belly-flopped into the water. Once again, the dogs failed to follow.

The river's current carried Sleepy downstream toward the cat on the overturned boat. Helped by the current at his back, Sleepy swam to the boat and climbed aboard. Izzy looked at him, and that was the only welcome he received from her. Sleepy shook some of the wetness from his coat, then stretched out on the deck so that the sun could dry the rest.

He kept his eyes on Izzy, but she kept hers on the hounds. The five dogs had finally decided to return home, and she watched them until they were just dots in the distance. Then the white cat stepped up to Sleepy and purred. He responded in kind.

Hours later, the private vessel of the two strays passed under a bridge. Dusk was on its way, and so were the last miles of the river, and so was the ocean.

8

HOME SWEET HOME

I T was late October now, and seven long weeks since Sleepy had disappeared from Walden. Despite offers of a free, purebred kitten from Mrs. Hall, no other cat had replaced him.

Her parents were quite willing for Cary to have the gift kitten. Indeed, Pop tried to persuade her several times. Remembering Sleepy's experiences with the snake and the strange dog, he didn't consider Walden any too safe without a cat.

But Cary clung stubbornly to the belief that Sleepy would return some day. She didn't know when, or how long it would take, but she was confident.

If the dogs at Walden missed the cat, they had no

way of telling Cary. Certainly their actions didn't indicate that they remembered their old friend. After the first week of Sleepy's absence, even Thumper stopped looking for him at mealtime and at night. The dog would cock his head and look wise when Cary mentioned Sleepy's name to him, but he didn't know what she was talking about. And the Lab pups, all sold and now in their new homes, had no memory of the day when the cat had saved their lives.

"I'm not just hoping that Sleepy will return," Cary confessed to her mother as the month neared its end. "I'm praying. First thing in the morning and the last thing at night."

Mom nodded in understanding, and smiled. She didn't say anything, but felt less foolish than before. She had been praying, too.

The object of their prayers had missed being swept into the ocean by thirty miles. The river current and the night wind had combined to push the craft ashore on the eastern bank of the river. Izzy had never been on that side of the river, but Sleepy had been born and raised there. Indeed, he was only fifteen miles from Walden, and could have reached home by dawn.

But the territory was as new and strange to Sleepy as it was to Izzy, and he was happy to follow her lead as she headed for the nearest cluster of lights. He may have sensed that she was a veteran stray and he was still a novice and had plenty to learn.

Izzy was a professional forager. The white lady cat could walk down a street at night and pick the one right house out of twenty that would offer overstuffed garbage cans or cans with loose tops or none at all. She knew that food stores were fine places to visit in the hour after dawn, and that the rear-door area was always more productive than the front. She preferred fish markets and never considered the danger of choking on a fish bone. Whenever she did swallow such bones, her digestive juices took care of them with ease.

She was a true artist at finding food in the wild. For the first time, Sleepy tasted such delicacies as wild grape, withered blueberries, and frog. One day, in an old orchard, they found the ground sprinkled with russet apples. On another day Izzy chased and captured a wounded pheasant. It was Sleepy's first taste of bird, and he didn't think very much of it. He almost choked on the feathers.

The roamers didn't know where they were and didn't care. Some days they traveled less than a mile, and on others they might cover ten, and quite often they ended up about where they'd started. The only place they stayed for two full days was at a dairy farm. The farmer didn't know how many cats he supported, and didn't have a name for a single one of them. But since they kept the rat and mice population at a minimum in his barns, he offered four huge pans of fresh, warm milk every day. That was the only place Izzy and Sleepy tasted milk.

They weren't the only strays wandering about the country. In fact, it was a rare day when they didn't see other vagabonds in the fields and woods. But they seemed to be the only pair. The others were always singles.

And then, in a way that Sleepy couldn't fathom, he and the white stray became the next thing to singles. It happened a week after their vacation at the dairy farm. For almost twenty minutes the two cats had been stalking a rabbit. The long-eared prey was aware of Sleepy and kept hopping away from the gray and white. He didn't know Izzy existed until he retreated around a bush and almost bumped into her. She broke his neck and was already tearing at his skin when Sleepy arrived on the scene to claim his share of the dinner.

Izzy snarled and spat at him. The astonished Sleepy backed off a few feet. They'd shared many a rabbit and a couple of woodchucks, and always before she'd welcomed him as a dinner companion.

Izzy's sudden, angry mood was both natural and normal. In a few days she would be ready for romance, but until the right time arrived she wanted nothing to do with Sleepy or any other tom.

Now she was nervous and tense, and not very hungry. She meowed loud enough for Sleepy to hear her, walked to a big rock, leaped to its top, and started to wash herself.

Sleepy waited a few minutes before walking to

the rabbit. He kept his eyes on Izzy every step of the way, as if expecting another attack from her. Sleepy was pleased to discover that she'd left plenty of meat for him, but Izzy continued to drive him away whenever he tried to approach her during all of that day and the next and the next. He followed her at a safe distance, and she made no attempt to lose him. At night they didn't huddle together for warmth, as they'd always done before. But each dawn he had no trouble finding her.

On the fourth morning Sleepy couldn't see her or hear her. All day long he stayed close to the spot in the woods where he'd slept during the night, but that didn't help. Izzy didn't return.

He didn't eat or drink. He didn't even try to find food or water. He was all alone again. Night had barely started when he climbed a tree, sat on a fat limb, and started to sing. His caterwauls were so sad, or so horrible, that even the owls remained silent. And although his sounding had nothing to do with it, rain started to fall.

Sleepy left his perch and started for the ground. He was halfway to the ground when he stopped and listened. Somebody was calling to him. Was that somebody Izzy?

She was calling to him, and she was also calling to all other interested toms within her vocal range. The time was right for Izzy. She was now in the mood for romance.

The big gray and white dropped to the ground, then hurried off in the direction of her calls. She

was less than three miles away and sitting on the
roof of a rusty, dented, wheel-less Cadillac. It was
the finest vehicle in an auto junk yard.

A blinking neon sign splashed light over the junk
yard. Four old toms were present by the time
Sleepy arrived, and all were waiting for trouble to
start. They understood the rules of the game. And
so did Sleepy. This time he didn't walk into a trap.
His approach to the Cadillac was a cautious one—a
slow step at a time, with a look around after each
step. When he was sure that his rivals numbered
only four, he went into action.

The smallest tom present was only ten feet away.
Sleepy crouched, sent a growl in the tom's direction, then leaped for him. The gray and white fell
short of his target. But the leap had been designed as
a feint. Sleepy turned, leaped again, and came down
on top of the biggest tom—a brown tabby who was
superior to his attacker in height, weight, and
reach. The surprised tabby went to the ground and
came up snarling and fighting, but he never had a
chance. He was soft from easy living, and the
younger Sleepy was lean and hard from life on the
road.

The battle lasted less than two minutes. The
tabby fought only to get his legs under him, then
fled into the rainy night. The conqueror looked
around for the other three toms, but they had seen

enough and had already retired from the scene.

And Izzy had seen enough, too. She jumped from the car roof to the hood to the ground. She walked to her companion of many days and rubbed against him, purring all the while. Sleepy had never heard such sweet purrs, and he tried to return the compliment by purring just as sweetly. She moved back and forth in front of him, tickling his nose with her tail on every turn. The lady was flirting with him and he responded.

They mated in the rain on the muddy ground of the auto junk yard. Not the most romantic spot in the world, but the setting didn't concern them.

And then, as if every lady on earth has a perfect right to change her mind, Izzy's mood changed. She screamed and turned on her mate, biting and slashing away with her claws.

The surprised Sleepy backed off. She came right after him, but he didn't try to fight back. He was as surprised as the tabby had been, and if he hadn't ducked and squirmed during his retreat, he'd have received just as severe a beating.

Izzy's fury lasted only a few minutes. When it was spent, she turned and walked away. A snarl was her parting remark.

Sleepy waited, then followed her at a safe distance. He was bewildered. What had he done?

Scientists couldn't have told him. They believe that the mating act produces severe pain for the lady cat, but they aren't certain. In any event, the lady always turns on the tom, as if it's the natural thing to do.

The gray and white's confusion lasted for several more days. He followed Izzy wherever she roamed, fought off several other toms who tried to win her favor, and never lost sight of her. But she kept her distance.

On the fifth day Izzy finally permitted him to come close. They were friends again, as they had been in all the weeks before she'd started acting in such a strange manner—strange to Sleepy, but not to her.

It was cold in the hills. For three bleak days in a row the northwest winds howled over the country-side. At Walden, Pop predicted that the earliest blizzard in history was in the making. He knew less about the weather than he did about cats, so Mom and Cary paid no attention to his prediction. Besides, who had ever heard of a blizzard at Thanksgiving time?

Sleepy and Izzy needed shelter from the foul weather. They had learned that the place to be was in a valley. The winds weren't as strong there, and the hunting was better. The mice, rabbits, and squirrels were more available, and Sleepy had acquired a taste for all.

Those were reasons enough for Izzy and Sleepy to linger in one place longer than usual. Their temporary home grounds were the shores of a small pond sheltered by woods. They had been in residence several days before they explored the north end of the pond and discovered the brook and the path leading off into the woods. To Izzy, the scenery was interesting and nothing more. She continued around the shore line, assuming that Sleepy would follow as usual.

But this time Sleepy was in no hurry to follow. The surroundings seemed familiar to him, as indeed they should have. Months before, he'd visited the spot many times with the Walden dogs and enjoyed a swim with them in the pond.

While Izzy sat and waited for him, he walked up the path and disappeared from her view. When he didn't reappear, she hurried after him. They progressed along the path, with Sleepy leading the way. For the first time since they'd been beached on the shore of the river, Sleepy was the leader. At long last the heralded homing instinct of *Felis catus* had clicked in the gray and white's brain. It happened when he was only a mile from home.

They reached the bottom of the cliff and followed the curved path upward to its brink. The path from there looked very familiar, and Sleepy hurried his pace. When he reached the open lawn, he bounded across it in the direction of the house.

That's when Izzy stopped. She stayed in the woods and climbed a tree. A people house wasn't the safest place to be around during daylight hours.

Her view from the tree didn't permit sight of Sleepy. He was out front on the terrace, and the house stood between them. The gray and white was meowing and scratching on the door, and the dogs inside were barking and dashing around. They were reacting as they had almost a year before when Sleepy's mother had appeared on the same terrace.

Mom was the only person present at Walden. She had just fed the kennel dogs and was coming up the drive, carrying the empty dog dishes. She heard the house dogs barking and wondered what had excited them.

When Mom saw Sleepy she couldn't believe her eyes. The dishes dropped from her hands and hit the drive. She stood there transfixed as Sleepy walked to her, rubbed against her legs, and purred. Finally she picked him up and rushed into the house. She plunked him down on the kitchen table, rushed to the phone, and dialed the Hall's number. That's where Cary was.

Billy's mother answered on the second ring, but Mom was still too stunned to say anything. "Hello, hello, hello, is anyone there?" asked Mrs. Hall. "Hello, hello?" she asked again before hanging up on her end.

So Mom had to dial again, and this time she was able to ask if Cary was still there.

"Yes?" asked Cary. "Is something wrong, Mom? I can hear the dogs barking."

The five dogs had discovered Sleepy. They were milling around the kitchen table, barking and whining. The cat was in a crouch and looking at them. He was the only calm individual present.

"Be quiet!" Mom shouted to the dogs. "No, not you, Cary."

"But what's wrong?"

"Nothing's wrong! Everything is right!" Mom shouted into the phone. "Guess what? Sleepy is home! Sleepy is home! You'd better come home right away!"

"I will. Goodbye," said Cary. She turned to Mrs. Hall and Billy and said, "I'm sorry, but I'll have to go home right away. I don't know what's wrong. The dogs were barking and Mom was shouting. I couldn't understand a word."

———

It was a gala day at Walden. If the house dogs resented all the special attention paid to Sleepy, they displayed it by almost ignoring him. They calmed down after the first few minutes. And while they may not have remembered him, the cat's scent must have seemed familiar and somehow safe.

"This is a fitting time for champagne," Pop announced at dinner. "Champagne for all of us, and for Sleepy, and for all the dogs. Too bad we don't have any." And as he climbed into bed that night, he remarked, "Think of it! Two thousand miles! Wow!"

"What two thousand miles wow?" asked Mom.

"Wait until the fellows at the office hear about this! Why, it will even take the wind out of Big Wind's sails! Think of it! Sleepy traveled two thousand miles to get home. I tell you, a cat's homing instinct is fabulous. Imagine, two thousand miles!"

"How can you know that?"

"He'd have been home sooner if the distance had been shorter," Pop assured her. "Looks a little thin, doesn't he? Why don't you give him some extra dog vitamins? I tell you, I was always sure that he'd find his way home!"

That wasn't true, of course, but Mom didn't argue about that or the two thousand miles. Sleepy was home, Cary was completely happy again, and nothing else really mattered. Now life at Walden could return to normal.

Mom didn't know, but she was in error. There was still a little problem named Izzy.

The white queen with the black ear would spend many more nights alone in the woods, but she could always count on a visit from Sleepy at dawn and several other times during the day. But he couldn't tempt her to the house. She knew dogs were there as well as people.

On several occasions he tried to bring food to her, but each attempt ended in failure. Twice he managed to steal chicken legs from the kitchen counter, but he couldn't find a way out of the house. Mom wondered why he'd turned into a food thief, for he was well fed. She suspected that he'd picked up some bad habits while away from home.

It didn't take long for the house dogs to know that there was a new stray cat in the woods. On wet mornings they never failed to pick up Izzy's scent near the cliff or below it. But while she saw them, they never saw her.

It was two weeks before Cary saw the newcomer. When Sleepy didn't appear at meal time, Cary went looking for him. From the brink of the cliff, she spotted him in the woods below with Izzy. The two cats were stalking something. When she called to Sleepy, the white cat ran off.

The first snow of December revealed the stranger's presence again. Around the general area of the cliff, Cary found the tracks of two cats. One set belonged to Sleepy, and she was sure that the smaller set had been made by the little white cat.

Cary showed the tracks to Billy Hall, and he guessed that the stranger was a female stray. "He wouldn't have a stray male for a friend," said the expert. "Males are loners."

On the school bus the next morning, Billy told Cary that he'd thought more about the white stray and reached some conclusions: "I think we can assume that Sleepy has been trying to steal food for his friend. And if this friend is a female, she may be more than a friend. Understand?"

"No."

"She may be his wife. And if she's carrying kittens, then she needs more food than usual, and hunting must be rough in the woods at this time of year."

It was a wasted school day as far as Cary was concerned. She couldn't concentrate on her studies. If Sleepy was destined to be a father, she didn't intend to have his children born in the woods. But first she knew she'd have to win his wife's trust, if that white cat was his wife. It was a problem, but Cary was determined to find a solution.

By the time she reached home that afternoon, Cary had devised a plan. It was a simple plan, so simple that she didn't discuss it with Billy for fear he'd think it was silly. But she did confide in her mother.

First she explained what she and Billy suspected: Sleepy was about to become a father, and the white stray would be the mother. "So if you don't mind, I intend to serve double rations to Sleepy every day, and I want to feed him near the cliff. If I don't stay too close, maybe she'll share his dinner and learn to trust me. Do you mind?"

"Certainly not!" Mom assured her. "Why, I'm thrilled at the prospect of having kittens around here. I've always adored kittens."

"What about Pop?"

"Let's wait until we're sure before telling him," her mother decided. "Then we'll wait a little longer. I'm afraid that he's still a one-cat man. Of course, that's an improvement. Maybe he'll improve some more."

Cary launched her plan that very afternoon. After the house dogs had been fed and had their romp, Cary and Sleepy headed for the cliff. The cat may have wondered why he hadn't been fed with the dogs, but he didn't complain, and he attacked his dinner dish as soon as his mistress placed it on the ground. It was the biggest meal she'd ever served him.

Cary didn't wait around that day to see what would happen. She knew that her cat wouldn't overeat, and that plenty of food would be left for his friend, or wife.

Sleepy returned to the house before the people sat down to dinner. His stomach wasn't bulging. The next morning when Cary retrieved his dinner dish, it was empty. And fresh tracks of the small cat were in the snow!

It was three days before Cary saw Izzy dining from her mate's dish, and five more until the pregnant stray didn't run when Cary came into view. After that, it was a question of how long it would take until the white queen would permit Cary to come close enough to touch her.

That momentous event didn't happen until Cary had started Christmas vacation. She had won Izzy's confidence, but surely some of the credit belonged to Sleepy. His complete trust in Cary must have influenced Izzy. The white stray was a copycat, not a fool.

On the following day, Billy Hall posted himself a hundred feet away and watched through binoculars as Cary picked up Izzy and held the cat in her arms. He was able to confirm what Cary already knew: Izzy would soon become a mother.

They named her Snow White Almost in honor of her black ear and tickings. Her nickname was Almost.

On the afternoon of Christmas Day, Billy Hall

visited Walden and requested a private conversation with Pop. They retired to Pop's study.

"This won't take long," Billy explained. "I bear good tidings."

"Thank you. And Merry Christmas to you, too, Billy," said Pop. "Is that all?"

"No, sir. You see, the women in your family have appointed me to inform you that you are about to become a grandfather."

Pop stared at the boy in disbelief. He sat down, gulped, and requested, "Would you repeat that, please?"

"Relatively speaking, you are about to become a grandfather."

Pop continued to stare at him, then asked, "Relatively?"

"Yes. Sleepy is about to become a father. In other words, there will soon be new kittens on earth."

Pop nodded in understanding and asked, "How soon?"

"We have no way of determining that, since the mating took place before Sleepy returned home with his wife. My mother thinks the happy event will take place in the next few days."

Pop was silent for almost a minute. He leaned back in his chair and gazed at the ceiling. Finally he said, "This is the first I knew about Sleepy being a married man. Would you mind filling me in?"

Billy gave his version of the story, and it was fairly accurate. He told of Cary's patience in winning the white queen's trust, and just why they had decided to name her Almost.

When he'd finished, Pop asked, "And where is Almost at this minute? Don't tell me that she's been hidden away in Cary's room?"

"No, she's in my home. We thought it would be best to have the kittening there, since new puppies are expected here sometime soon. And of course, we've been through many kittenings before."

"Very thoughtful of you, Billy. Thank you. And I can count on you to find good homes for the kittens?"

"They won't belong to me," said Billy. "They'll belong to Cary."

Pop shook his head and a puzzled expression appeared on his face. "Doesn't anyone understand?" he asked of the world in general. "If it took me more than forty years to accept one cat, how can I accept a dozen more overnight? No, no, I don't deserve this!"

Billy didn't correct him. Kittens rarely come by the dozen. The average litter runs from one to four kittens, but only a cat expert seems to know that.

So Pop, on the evening of December 28, was relieved to learn that the children of Sleepy and Almost had arrived that very afternoon and numbered only two. Two daughters, and one was forty-three minutes older than the other.

His wife told him the news at the dinner table, just before dessert was served. "The small one is black with a white chest, and the big one has markings similar to Sleepy's," she explained. "And Billy is being very helpful. He'll keep them for a few weeks, or until after our new pups are whelped."

"Fine," said Pop. "I'll inquire at the office and see who wants a kitten. Maybe Big Wind will take one."

Mom winked at Cary before replying, "We were thinking of keeping both Almost and her kittens. After all, Sleepy does need help. There are just too many moles and mice for one cat to handle. Would you mind bringing in the dessert, Cary?"

As soon as his daughter was out of hearing, Pop pointed at his wife and said, "Now listen to me! At this very moment we have enough non-self-supporting animals on this place for me to support. Three more cats is three cats too many! I realize I married an animal lover, and that my daughter inherited this love from you, but I want you to know that this is not Christmas Day! I'm not forgetting for one minute that you conned me into keeping Sleepy because he arrived here on Christmas! Well, this isn't Christmas! This is December 27, or 28, or 29, or something. A day without special meaning! What's this?"

The question referred to the object in Cary's hands. She was returning to the table and carrying a huge cake. It was a three-layer chocolate cake, with strawberry icing and sprinkled with coconut, cherries, raisins, and olives. Pop's favorite cake! On top and at its very center was a single, lighted candle.

As Cary placed the cake before her father, she

and her mother started to sing Happy Birthday. Their sweet voices inspired the house dogs. All five Labradors trotted into the room and started to howl. Sleepy walked into the room as the singing and then the howling ended. He didn't add to the noise.

The head of the house had forgotten his own birthday!

"You may not think that today, December 28, is a special day, but I do, and Cary does, and so do the dogs and Sleepy," said Mom. And then, just to make sure that he got the point, she added, "All of us think that your birth date is just as important and as special as Christmas. Make a wish now and blow out the candle."

Pop closed his eyes, opened them, leaned forward, and blew out the candle.

"What was your wish?" asked Cary.

Her father looked at her and smiled. "I wished," he said, "that you and your mother will not decide to raise kangaroos. I understand that those beasts dine exclusively on caviar."

Four weeks later, Almost and her infant daughters joined Sleepy at Walden. It was the start of community living for three families: a cat family, a dog family, and a human family.

All three lived in harmony, and they still do.

On a snowy Christmas day, Cary and her five dogs unexpectedly find a gray and white kitten at the front door. Billy Hall, eighth grade classmate and local cat expert, offers Cary advice on how to care for the hungry and wet little cat.

Cary names the kitten "Sleepy" and tries to persuade Pop to let Sleepy stay. The family has always preferred dogs, so this is no easy task. After the kitten encounters a variety of adventures with toads, deer, snakes, stray cats, and a vicious wild dog, Pop begins to weaken.

Just as Sleepy begins to win acceptance, he gets lost. His experiences in a new world of super-highways, city pounds, and unfriendly strangers is a lively and exciting story.

Cat lovers will especially appreciate the many interesting facts about the cat family which the author has interlaced throughout his story.

THE PRENTICE-HALL LIBRARY BINDING

The binding of this edition is guaranteed to last the life of the sheets. It is bound in durable, pyroxylin-impregnated, stain-resistant cloth, and is smythe sewn and reinforced with cloth hinges.

Ages 9 and up
Grades 4 and up